"What IS it?" Jane repeated, trying as unsuccessfully to stifle her laughter as she was in getting the thing off her husband.

"Well, you know… In that book you left on my nightstand… There was that one scene you had marked, and, well, you said,"

"I said read it, not reenact it! Gosh, Charlie – you look ridiculous! And I didn't mean that part anyway. You were supposed to read two paragraphs down from there."

"You're the one who placed the sticky note! How was I supposed to know what paragraph?"

"Well, how was I supposed to know you'd pull a stunt like this?"

#25Reasons

Why Charlie

Should Never

Read Jane's Books to Jane

Also by Phyl Campbell

For Teens and Adults

>Mother Confessor One

>Mother Confessor Two

>The Carley Patrol

For Children

>Martha's Chickens and the Pirates

Nonfiction

>Confessions of a Grammar Enthusiast

#25 Reasons Why Charlie Should Never Read Jane's Books to Jane

By Phyl Campbell

Twenty-five Reasons
Why Charlie Should Never Read Jane's Books to Jane

#25 Reasons Why Charlie Should Never Read Jane's Books to Jane / Phyl Campbell

ISBN 13: 978-1505924435
ISBN 10: 150592443X

Printed in the United States of America

Romantic Comedy: Jane's plan to engage her husband in more romantic acts has numerous disastrous consequences.

1.Housewives: Fiction. 2. Rural Suburban Life: Fiction

To all the Charlies who try -- and fail -- in hilarious miserable ways – and to the women who refuse to give up on them or accept less from them.

Read me this passage in bed and I will wear a teddy – and I don't mean the stuffed animal.

A Night that Ends Badly

"'Even before she could scream out in ecstasy, he plunged into her and touched his fangs to the throbbing pulse of her throat. She said...'"

"What? What did she say?" Jane cried, bordering on ecstasy herself. She'd had this great idea to have Charlie read to her in bed from her favorite books. She hadn't read this one; she'd checked it out on recommendation from a friend and put it on Charlie's pile without thinking. The premise was good. Sexy vampires and hot women. She was in bed with Charlie. She was scantily clad in a black silk teddy. He was reading in just a pair of boxers – ready for the words on the page to get them both in the mood. Charlie was reading to her. She was relaxed. She felt so turned on.

"Wait a minute." Charlie said. "I've got to blow my nose."

"Ewww gross." Jane complained. The great mood she had was evaporating by the second. "Now? You have to do that now?"

"You don't want my snot on the pages of your bodice ripper, do ya?" Charlie blew his nose rather loudly into the handkerchief he kept on the nightstand, next to a pile of fingernail clippings and several empty soda cans.

"Argh! Never mind!" Jane rolled over, silk teddy fully obscured by the plum comforter. If he hadn't suspected that sex was no longer on the table, he better take the hint -- quickly.

That was the first reason why Charlie should never read Jane's books to Jane.

When he got home from school the next afternoon, fourteen year old Seth found his mother sitting curled up on the couch with a blanket tucked around her legs. In one hand was her favorite pen. In the other was a pad of sticky notes. The look of concentration on his mother's face should have been a clue to leave her alone, but he was her son. Violating her private space was part of the job. Always had been. Seth didn't know why his mother loved sticky notes, but she used them everywhere. On his bathroom mirror, his mother had posted: "eat breakfast; brush teeth; brush hair; apply deodorant." It wasn't that Seth forgot to do these things. It was that he was fourteen and he didn't want to. But his mother put those things on a sticky note and then told him to check it. Yep, the sticky note was still there, on the bathroom mirror -- check. She also put stickies in his lunch. Seth might find one on his napkin suggesting that he "use on face before tossing." He might find one on the inner lid reminding him to meet with his tutor after school or to turn in lunch money. Seth saw the sticky notes as little mother's helpers -- nagging him throughout the day in her absence.

But he knew his mother made other lists on sticky notes. When his mom wasn't reading or driving him somewhere, she was making lists. Even more often than the lists she left for him, Seth's mother was making lists for herself. Books to read, places to take him, bills to pay, errands to run, websites to explore.

If Seth had X-ray vision, he would have seen that the current list went something like this:

Pokes fun at foreplay ideas
No camera ready-physique
Thinks manscaping is something done outdoors
Thinks toothpaste and deodorant are optional
Snores
Doesn't bring home flowers
Doesn't clean up after himself

Since Seth didn't have X-ray vision, and there were rules about reading over his mother's shoulder without her permission, he just asked her, "Whatcha writing, Mom?"

"A list of your father's shortcomings."

Score! Dad was in the doghouse. "Did you put that he snores?" *Sorry Dad, but it's you or me and I don't want it to be me.*

"Number five."

"Good. But should be number one. And he's getting a little bald."

Jane put down her pen and looked into her son's smirking face. "Hey. That's your father you're talking about."

"I'm just saying." Seth's face was all innocence.

"I know what you're *just saying*, Seth. I'm *just saying* I wonder what your room looks like."

"It looks like a room. You've seen it, Mom. It has four walls, a ceiling, and a floor with a bed and stuff."

"Exactly. About that stuff."

"Take the hint and go clean your room, sport." Charlie came in the front door, crossed to the couch, pointed a disappointed Seth in the direction of his room, and kissed Jane on the top of her head – all without missing a beat. "Hi, honey."

"Hi."

#25 Reasons

"Another list?"

"Seemed like a good idea."

"Do I want to know?"

"Absolutely not."

"It's about you, Dad!" Seth shouted back down the stairs on route to his room. "She says you're short, bald, and fat!"

"Nice try, buddy." Charlie called back good-naturedly. "I'm still on her side."

Jane chuckled as Seth groaned the rest of the way to his room. Charlie eased himself onto the couch next to Jane. She wiggled her toes underneath his leg, anger evaporating.

"How was work?" she asked.

"Same old, same old. Seth?"

"Full of himself. He got a B plus on his very first ninth grade science report."

"Great!" Charlie's eyes twinkled. "Which website did he download it from?"

Jane frowned. "Not funny, Charlie. Seth worked really hard on that paper."

"And you worked really hard keeping him on track."

"It took him three hours. I could have done it myself in ten minutes."

"I'm proud of your restraint. We'll celebrate with ice cream after dinner. How about your other thing – any luck with the job search?"

Jane propped her elbow on the back of the couch and supported her curly head with one hand. "Not unless I want to work nine to five Monday through Friday for minimum wage or pull an MBA out of my butt for a dollar an hour more."

Charlie mirrored his wife's position. "I thought you were only looking at part time?"

As he put his hand to his head, Jane couldn't help but notice how much his hairline had receded since they first met. And Jane knew behind that hand, the hair Charlie was losing up top was find a new home growing out his eyebrows and ears. Not that she considered herself anything special in the looks department. Donuts had generously agreed to stay with her and make sure she never lost the baby weight. The auburn hair that she'd celebrated as a college student was more silver than brown now. She often thought about dying it, but Charlie didn't like the smell of harsh chemicals, and who was she trying to impress, anyway? She knew how old she was.

"I am. But all part time includes weekends now, I guess."

"That's not going to work."

#25 Reasons

"Yeah, and neither am I, apparently."

"Well, one of us needs to be home when Seth gets here. I suppose I could ask my boss --"

"No way. Hard enough to have me looking for work. Don't need to give anyone a reason to put you out of a job as well."

"Which is why you don't have to work. I make enough. We have a roof over our heads. It'll be all ours -- in just three hundred forty more completely reasonable low monthly payments."

"And then we die and they bury us here."

"Oh, talk dirty to me."

"I know we're doing all right." Jane reached out a hand and placed it on Charlie's shoulder. "I just know two incomes – like two heads – are better than one. Wouldn't it be nice to own this house in just a hundred and seventy completely reasonable monthly payments?" She grinned.

"Then we could buy a boat." Charlie grinned, too.

"Charlie."

"I could teach you to ski."

"Charlie!"

"Teach you how to ski so you can show off a cute little bikini." Charlie teased.

"Tankini at least. Shirt and shorts probably. No one needs to see that much of me." Jane adjusted the blanket

9

around her legs and tucked the ends under her armpits self-consciously. She had never been a twig, but the extra pounds she'd put on since she was pregnant could hardly be attributed to baby weight alone. Years of marriage had been generous – especially to her waistline. Her brand of feminism dictated that Charlie love her for her mind and not her body. To her frequent surprise and disbelief, Charlie loved both.

"Let Seth take the wheel so I can see that much of you."

"Get run aground by the teen boat driver and then get eaten by sharks."

"Not in freshwater."

"Besides, I'd rather have horses."

"OK. So after I get my boat, you can have some horses."

"And a stable boy named Hans."

"Hans?" Charlie affected a Norwegian accent. "Sure, I've heard Hans is good with the horses, yah. But he's not as good as Heidi."

"Hey – you got your boat. Why do you need Heidi?"

"I think once you have my Hans on you, you won't care so much about the horses." Charlie wiggled his fingers suggestively, playing on the idea of a handy Hans.

"Do you promise to handle me, Hans?"

10

#25 Reasons

"Oh, Hans will handle you Jane. But then the horses will break loose and you will have to come away with me on my boat to evade police."

"Why am I evading police?"

"Because you ignored all the studs in your stable while Hans was handling you."

"So now the cops are jealous?"

"Very much so."

"What will you tell the police if they catch us?"

"Yes, officers, I am not being this Hans person. I am his brother Sven. Sven is much better in bed." Charlie took Jane's sticky notes and glanced at them as he leaned over Jane in a semi-seductive manner. "Sven can do the manly scaping and he only snores half the night."

"What does Sven do the other half of the night?"

"Sven makes love to beautiful women like Jane Hart." Charlie leaned the rest of the way into Jane. She didn't resist, and her lips met his. This was the Charlie she loved. Funny, sexy, and charming all at once. She pulled back to look into his face, then kissed him again. Charlie didn't seem to mind.

Seth chose that unfortunate moment to re-enter the living room and see his parents making out on the couch. "Ugh! Get a room, you two!"

"This is my room. They're all my rooms. Get your own house." Charlie said.

Charlie was teasing of course, but there was a bite to it. Jane mentally added "does not play well with others" as a potential eighth item on her list.

If only there was a way to make Charlie more like Hans. More like any hunk from the romances she devoured. Sure he was a good husband and a good father. Sure he still made her laugh. Still, she was unsettled. Surely this was not the best she was ever going to get.

The first year they were married, Jane thought it would be helpful to buy Charlie a copy of *Romance for Dummies*. He retaliated with a copy of the *Kama Sutra*. She couldn't be direct and he wouldn't get subtle. So she thought maybe she could resort to bribery. She put suggestive titillating sticky notes marking favorite passages in favorite romance novels. She had hoped more than once that if he just read what she read, just a little, some of that romance would rub off on him. He had thumbed through a few of the novels before agreeing to her terms. She hadn't realized his vitriol for vampire romance when she added the unread book to the stack. She didn't understand; he was fine with Stephenie Meyer. But last night's sick vampire sucked the life out of Jane's libido. Charlie hadn't so much as sniffled all day. Then it was time for bed and reading and just a few pages in – because of course Charlie didn't start at the beginning -- his plague hit. So gross!

Most of the time, Jane could ignore Charlie's side of the bed. But when Charlie protested via his bodily functions – excessive farting, plague-like flu symptoms, freakishly long fingernails – her personal brand of heroin became her personal brand of kryptonite. Jane went from carnal lust to reminding herself that Arkansas had capital punishment and she looked terrible in orange. Worse, she couldn't tell how much Charlie did on purpose compared to actual psycho-somatic symptoms. She could hardly blame him for becoming flatulent when he was disgusted. He couldn't blame her for the migraines she got from his flatulence. That either condition made love-making impossible was just a sign of getting older, right?

Jane sighed. Most of her single friends – and half her married ones – thought Charlie was a great catch. So why did Jane feel so stuck?

If luck
favors the prepared,
do you feel like
trying yours?

Unwanted Advances

Charlie Hart came home to find Jane and Seth sitting at the kitchen table. Seth's back was to him. He caught Jane's eye and raised an eyebrow.

"Seth, do you want to show your Dad what you got at school today?"

Charlie was just about to ask if Seth had gotten a hickey or an F when his son stood up and turned to face him, a bag of ice on his face. "What have you got there, son?"

Seth lowered the bag. His right eye was swollen and all kinds of purple.

Charlie whistled. As far as shiners went, Seth's was a thing of beauty. He looked at Jane as Seth sat back down. "Why didn't you call me?"

"I didn't even know about it until a little bit ago, Charlie. And I'm still working out the details."

Charlie pulled up a chair to join his wife and son at the table. His own troubles would just have to wait. "So what teeth have you pulled so far?"

"Apparently, Frank called one of Seth's friends a name, and Seth told him to take it back."

15

"Huh? A little teasing is good among the guys, don't you think, Seth? What did Frank call the other guy? Was it Trevor? They're always messing around."

"Susan." Seth said quietly.

"Frank called Trevor 'Susan?' " Well, I guess that's…"

Seth looked at his mother with obvious daggers for his clueless dad. Jane very calmly said, "No, Charlie. Susan was the friend Frank called a name. Apparently, it rhymes with 'hunt.' "

Charlie was stunned. What were middle-school students doing calling each other names like that?

Seth didn't understand his father's silence. "Frank was being a total perv, Dad. He was popping the back of Susan's bra at lunch until she got up and moved, and when she got up, he called her – that word – in front of everyone. I didn't even know what it meant, but Susan looked ready to cry so I told him to take it back. Then he called me a faggot and punched me."

"Why that little"

"Uh, he's not little, Dad. He plays football. When he wouldn't take it back and I tried to body slam him, I don't think he even felt anything." Seth slumped back down at the table. Jane stood behind him, rubbing his shoulders.

Charlie stood there scratching his head, trying to let everything sink in. He gave up and sank into another chair at the table. Their kitchen table had seen a lot of bumps and bruises, permanent marker artwork and rings from beverages without coasters. The wood had been solid for over a decade. It would hold him up through this.

"OK. So name calling by him, interference by you, eye punching by him, body slamming by you. Did anyone else get involved?"

"Well, the football coach had lunch duty, so when he asked Frank what was going on, I think Frank said I tripped and fell into his fist on accident."

"You think? What did you say?"

"Not much. I was on the floor."

"I see."

"I have half a mind to go up there and talk to the principal about what he lets that coach and his precious players get away with!" Jane fumed.

"No, Mom! That will only make things worse! Susan's already mad at me."

"Mad at you? Why is Susan mad at you? You were defending her."

"She said she was handling it and could take care of herself. She said she did not approve of my," Seth threw up air quotes, " 'macho display.' "

"Why was Frank even sitting by you?"

17

"The cheerleaders were mad at him, so they told him he had to sit at the loser's table.

"You're not a loser!"

"It's OK, Mom. It just means nerds."

"Are you hearing this, Charlie?"

Charlie shook his head. "It stinks, but it's a lot like crap we put up with in school."

"Seth should not have to put up with crap at school. Not with all the anti-bullying, inclusiveness training seminars, and all the other parent-teacher crap I've had to sit through! Seth should be benefitting from everything we've been through."

Whether embarrassed, angry, or just bored, Seth took some invisible cue to jump up and leave the room.

"Seth? Where are you going? This conversation isn't over."

"Let him be for a bit, Charlie."

"Do we need to sign him up for karate or self-defense classes or something?"

"I think that would just put gasoline on the match, Charlie. I just wish the school would take better care of my baby."

"You better not call him your baby or he'll definitely keep getting his ass handed to him."

#25 Reasons

"I know. I don't. But we're home now. That's part of what kills me. I was in the PTA room making calls for this fundraiser thing. I was in the building when this happened – and no one thought to let me know my kid was unconscious on the cafeteria floor."

Charlie blew out a frustrated laugh. "Jane, I know you want to believe that the world is a beautiful place. And I love how you believe that people are basically good and decent individuals. But people are just trying to give as they think they're getting, and for a lot of people, that's just getting screwed over."

"That's cynicism for you."

"That's reality. Look, the girl – Sharon."

"Susan."

"Right, Susan -- she didn't even appreciate what Seth did for her. Probably, if it had been us twenty years ago, you would have did the same thing she did. Frank is the only one who did what society expected."

"So that's it? That's where we're supposed to leave it?"

"Fight it all you want to, Jane. Be proud of Seth for doing the same. But yeah. The world's basically messed up and not getting any better."

"That may be the saddest thing I ever heard."

"Remember that when I'm reading to you tonight. This. This conversation, right now, is the saddest thing you ever heard."

Charlie knew better than to look at Jane. Still, he took his foot and stuck it in further. If he was going to get a dig in about Jane's stupid books, he better do it while she was more focused on Seth.

"You're a feminist. Susan's a feminist. Men like Seth and me, we don't get it. You want us to help you, but then you don't want our help. You want me to respect you as a feminist but you want me to read this crap to you, too. Therefore, Frank is the only one who did what makes sense. You can always count on a stupid bully to be a stupid bully."

"This is not about the books. This is about our son."

"The hell it's not about the books. It's about you women and simple guys like Seth and I trying to figure you out."

"Me." Jane corrected softly.

"Me, what?"

"Simple guys like Seth and me."

"Fine. Seth and me. I think Seth and ME need to go out for a couple of steaks and then maybe some ice cream." Charlie called out "What do you think, son, would steak and ice cream work on that bruise of yours?"

#25 Reasons

"I'm coming!" came the disembodied reply.

"We're not going for ice cream. You promised we'd turn in early tonight."

"I promised to be more romantic. I promised to try. I still get dinner and I never expected our kid to have a shiner the size of a dinner plate. So we'll go out. We'll have a nice dinner. We'll get home in plenty of time for me to spend another night gagging over one of your books."

"You used to like it when I read them."

"I still do -- like YOU -- AFTER YOU read them. I don't like it when I read them. The books are still crap."

"Don't. Diss. My. Books."

"You can hardly call them books. And certainly not literature."

"Charlie!"

"So, are we going?" Seth asked from the stairs. He picked up a hoodie from the bottom step, sniffed it, and then pulled it on over his head. His shoelaces were loose and dangling.

"We're not going out. Your dad was just being a tease."

"Oh, man!" Seth whined.

"Oh, no. I never tease about ice cream. We are definitely getting ice cream."

"And steak?" Seth asked hopefully.

21

"Yes. Steak. Steak first or dessert first?"

"Steak with a milkshake for a drink?"

"You got it kid. Anything you want."

"What about what I want?" Jane protested.

"Later, later. We'll do that, too. Maybe I can get the ice cream to numb my brain enough to think that I'm reading something good."

Jane rolled her eyes and grabbed her jacket as she followed her men out the door.

Maybe this
warrants a
skinny dip in
the lake?

Love in the Great Outdoors

"We're going camping." Jane announced Friday night after dinner. "We'll leave tomorrow and head to the campsite, go fishing at the lake, eat a picnic lunch, and then have fish we catch for dinner. Sunday morning we'll eat a campfire breakfast, and then we'll head home unless you want to rent a boat and take it out."

"Ok." Charlie said noncommittally from his armchair, laptop in his lap.

"Oh, man. Why do we have to go anywhere?" Seth barely looked up from his wireless controller. The "mission" was still going strong, with twelve kills already registered. His eye was mostly yellow now, but Jane thought it was one more reason to get her son away from the video games and involved in real activity.

"We spend too much time in front of our electronics and not enough time bonding as a family. You both got fishing licenses for

Christmas from Grandpa. Shouldn't you at least use them once before it gets too cold?"

"But I can fish anytime I want to!" Seth complained. "I have the game and the pole. Dad can do it with me." During the entire complaint, the A and B buttons did not miss a click. "Gotcha!"

"Fishing on your video game is NOT enjoying the fresh air of the great outdoors. C'mon. You used to beg us to take you fishing."

"But Amos said he might be doing an online tournament Sunday."

"And Amos is probably getting told that he is spending Sunday with his family. Just like you."

"Who's Amos?" Charlie asked, looking up from his laptop with concern.

"Just a classmate, Charlie. It's Ok. I think we saw Amos at the mall the other day after school. Is that right, Seth?"

"Yeah. He and Drew were both there."

"Who's Drew? I feel like I don't know any of his friends, anymore, Jane."

Jane knew Charlie was worried because his eyes hadn't returned to his personal screen. She tried to reassure him. "The friends you know are still his friends, Charlie. But he's not in elementary school – or even middle school – anymore. He's a bigger fish swimming in a bigger pond these days. That's all. You're not missing out." But she knew he was, in a way. She took for granted all the things she knew about their son because she was home with him in the hours between school and dinner. Charlie missed a lot of that, and wasn't happy about it.

"I'm missing out if I can't do the tournament with Amos and Drew." Seth complained, oblivious to the separate world his parents were commiserating in.

"No Seth. And that's my final word. But we can, and we are, going camping this weekend. Am I understood?"

"Yes ma'am." Charlie and Seth both answered sheepishly.

"Any pertinent questions?"

"No, ma'am."

"Great. I'm going to make some sandwiches for our lunch tomorrow. Seth, would you bring the cooler in? It's on the shelf in the garage."

Seth started to growl his displeasure, but Charlie caught his eye and he instantly thought better of it. He got up to do what he was told.

Charlie got up and stood behind his wife, who had busied herself getting bologna and mayo from the fridge and bread from the pantry and was hurriedly slapping mayo and was now creating an assembly line for sandwich making.

"You don't even like fishing." He said quietly in her ear.

"You do. And I love you." Jane replied matter-of-factly while continuing the assemblage of ingredients.

"You're not planning to throw us overboard and leave us to drown, are you?"

"Don't be silly! You've been saying for ages that we need to do this. Let's do this."

"What are you going to do while we're fishing?"

"I don't know. If you get a boat I might go out with you. If you stay on shore I can talk to you. I might set up the tent first, though."

#25 Reasons

"Oh, Jane – you don't want to do that by yourself. Seth and I will help you. I want us to stay together. "

"Alright then. Then, I might bring a book. Anything I should bring to read out loud to you and Seth? Something that might bore the fish into submission?"

"Why not get one of your books where they're getting busy in the woods?"

"Because most of those end up with someone getting killed. Indoors, or in fields, those are the places where my heroines are safe. I'm certainly not reading the other kind while we're out camping. I'm paranoid enough."

"What are you going to do if we encounter another spider?"

"Scream like a girl and get rescued by my husband."

"Thank you." Charlie nuzzled and kissed his wife's neck.

"Don't thank me until you've had one of my amazing sandwiches." Jane replied.

"Well, if you insist." Charlie snatched a sandwich off the pile.

"Hey, those are for the picnic!" Jane cried.

"But I'm hungry and I had to make sure they were tasty. They are. Quite." Charlie smiled while smacking his lips. "Did you make the mayo yourself?"

"Yeah. I did it yesterday. So much better than the store bought stuff."

"Well, great. Thanks, honey."

"No problem."

"Where is Seth with the cooler?"

"Here!" Seth struggled with his cumbersome load.

"What in the world? Seth, it's not that heavy. What is in this?" Jane started to take the cooler from her son, then, realizing he wasn't making up his strain, popped open the lid. A sour smell made them all gag almost immediately.

"Oh my word, Seth. Set it down. Set it down!"

"Oops." Seth looked sheepishly at his dad.

"Did you not unload it from the last time we used it?"

"I thought it was just bottles of water."

#25 Reasons

"And your chocolate milk pet, from the smell of it."

"Oops." Seth couldn't decide whether his mistake was gross or funny, and didn't want any more electronics time taken away. So he said as little as possible and hoped for the best.

"We'll put some baking soda in it tonight and see if that takes care of it. Put the chocolate milk bottle into the outside trash can, please."

"OK. Sorry, Mom."

"It happens, Seth. If I thought it was just water in the cooler, and I was strong enough to lift it over my head and put it on the shelf, I might have."

"I am getting very strong."

"Yeah, buddy. Go shower. You stink!" Charlie teased.

"Dad!"

Jane got the baking soda. Charlie started to help her remove the water bottles, but Jane stopped him.

"I'm doing this for you, Charlie. I've got this."

"Ok. But I don't mind helping my wife."

"And I suspect I'll need more help. Like with the tent and stuff. There will be plenty of things to do tomorrow. Seth will be less helpful than you for a lot of them."

"It's too bad Seth can't be in his own tent."

"Charlie." Jane had bought Seth a new pup tent, but she didn't want to ruin the surprise yet.

"I could make you howl and we'd tell him it was wolves."

"Oh, you are bad." Jane laughed.

"If I agree, will you spank me?"

"Eww! Eww! Eww! Do you two have to be so gross every time I walk into the room?"

"Parenting 101. Embarrass the teenager."

"Uh huh. It's in the handbook."

"Real mature guys." Disgusted, Seth left.

The next morning, Seth greeted his parents with a "let's get this over with," but even he couldn't hide the grin when Jane showed him his new tent. The drive to the campsite was relatively drama free. Tents were erected, and there was plenty of time for Charlie to rent a small boat and take his family out on the lake.

#25 Reasons

True to her word, Jane had brought reading material. Nothing too titillating for the fish, but Charlie had seen something slightly more scandalous in her backpack. He simultaneously hoped that he wouldn't have to read it and that she would. All sorts of good things happened when Jane read her sexy books.

Still, he didn't complain too much when it was dark and Jane invited him to their tent. Seth was outside with the dying campfire, roasting the last marshmallows. Charlie had set a pair of filled two-gallon water jugs, never opened, next to Seth just in case the fire flared. Son occupied, Charlie accepted the book Jane offered him and was rewarded to see that she wasn't wearing much other than her blanket. And she'd zipped their sleeping bags together. Then he looked at the title.

"*Her Hooded Cloak?* Is this a Red Riding Hood story?"

"You said you wanted to make me howl."

Charlie snorted, but doffed his clothes quickly and snuggled in beside Jane.

"She better not be mistaking the wolf for Grandma."

"She doesn't."

"Hmmm. 'While on the way to her grandmother's cottage, Riding Hood met a dark, handsome stranger in the wood. His black lambskin coat shone devilishly even without the aid of sunlight in the dark wood.'"

"Mmm." Jane purred. "Sounds dangerous."

Charlie skipped ahead a little, and continued to read.

"Let's see. 'My, what a big member you have.' 'The better to pleasure you with, my dear.'"

"I'm so glad Seth has his own tent."

"Speaking of – listen to him out there."

Charlie closed the book and they both listened to the teen who thought he had privacy. "And with my magic wand, I will roast a marshmallow and write my name – all at the same time. I'm even going to use cursive, folks!" Seth continued in a hushed announcer voice. "The crowd goes 'ooh.'" Then, in a louder announcer voice, Seth said, "Are you nervous, Mr. Hart?"

And Seth replied to himself, "Of course not, Mr. Hart. I do this every day. Twice on Sundays." "But a lot of people are watching." "The more the merrier! OK, folks! Here goes nothing! S. E. T. – oops!"

"Why did he say 'oops'?" Jane asked.

"Uh, Mom?" Charlie jumped up and struggled into a pair of pants despite not being the requested parent.

"Charlie – why did he say 'oops'?"

"Dad?" Seth's voice betrayed a rising level of panic. Charlie unzipped the flap and swore.

"Charlie, what is that smell?" Jane had a bad feeling, and she didn't want to confirm it with her own eyes. Nor did she want to leave the warm blankets she was naked under.

"Mom!"

"I'm here, Seth." Charlie said. "Dad's here."

"Charlie? Is something on fire? Charlie!"

"Seth! Stop making it worse!"

"I didn't mean to!"

"Hand me one of the water jugs."

Seth handed him one. It was empty.

"Where's the water?"

Phyl Campbell

"I got thirsty."

Charlie didn't have time to process this.

"What about the water in the cooler?"

"Uh." Seth was again at a loss for words.

"Run down to the lake and bring back a bucket of water."

"OK." Seth started to go. "Where's a bucket?"

"In the boat."

"Oh." Seth ran.

Charlie grabbed the cooler of ice and sodas and dumped it on Seth's pup tent. "I hope your backpack is waterproof, kid, and your phone is in its case."

"Do I need to come out there?" Jane called from inside the tent.

"I got it." Charlie called.

He could see Jane getting up anyway. He knew curiosity would get the better of her. But he preferred her in the tent, naked.

"How bad is it?" She asked a few minutes later, still buttoning her shirt as she exited the tent.

#25 Reasons

"Well, I hope you kept the receipt." Charlie tried to laugh.

"Where's Seth?"

"I sent him down to get a bucket of water."

"Guess you didn't need it."

"He was fanning the flames with all his dancing around. Can you believe he drank four gallons of bottled water – and left the sports bottles in the cooler?"

"Sounds about right."

"I honestly do not understand that boy."

"Well, his tent is ruined. At least he wasn't in it. I guess he'll have to share ours."

"Oh, no." Charlie said. "No way. We did the book thing. I did my part. We had a deal. Seth can sleep under the stars or in the truck. There is no way I am sharing my tent with the kid!"

Seth came up the hill empty-handed.

"Where's the bucket of water, son?"

"Couldn't find the bucket."

"Couldn't find it in the boat? The white bucket?"

"I looked all over."

"Uh huh."

"Seth," Jane intervened. "Go find the white bucket under the third seat behind the fishing lures and bring it back."

"OK, Mom." Seth went trotting back down to the beach.

"He's not going to find it." Charlie said.

"Oh, I forgot to tell him to put water in it." Jane chided herself aloud, ignoring Charlie's comment.

"Why does it matter, the fire's out? But he's not going to"

"Found it!" Seth's voice rang out.

"Son of a"

"Yeah, don't finish that. You know very well whose son he is." Jane smiled smugly and retreated to the tent while Charlie seethed.

"Here's the bucket, Dad." Seth called. "What should I do with it?"

Charlie had the strong urge to turn the bucket over and give his son a hat. He fought the urge.

"Oh, look. The fire's out. Oh, man! My backpack!" Seth swooped down over the sodden remains and lifted the backpack out of the tent.

#25 Reasons

He fished into the side pocket, dug out his phone, and swiped at the screen. "Good. It still works!"

Charlie's withering look might have melted the device, but Seth didn't notice it.

"So now what, Dad?"

"Mom's going to get you an extra blanket from our tent, and you're going to sleep in the bed of the truck."

"The bed of the truck? Oh, man!" Seth groused.

Jane's hand appeared through the tent flap with the blanket and a pillow. Seth huffed while putting them in the truck bed, and because the truck was parked right next to Charlie and Jane's tent, his every noise of teenage drama was broadcast to his parents. The metal sides of the truck bed only amplified the sound.

"You two aren't doing lovey dovey crap, are you?"

"Go to sleep, Seth." Jane called. "Does he have his earbuds?" She whispered to Charlie. "Maybe you should move the truck."

"It'll be fine." Charlie said irritably.

"Seth, do you have your earbuds?" Jane called out anyway.

"Shoot! My earbuds!" Seth hopped over the side of the truck and ran back to the tent. "Oh, man! Mom, the fire burned my buds!"

"You'll live." Jane called.

"Unless I kill him," Charlie muttered.

"I heard that. I'm calling Child Protective Services." Seth called.

"Daddy loves you, Seth. Sorry about your earbuds. Try to go to sleep anyway."

"He was fine until you reminded him."

"I know. But I thought you wanted to"

"I'm not listening!"

"We're not talking to you, Seth."

"Yeah, but you're being gross."

"Maybe we should let him sleep in the cab with the radio." Jane whispered.

"Yeah, that'd be awesome! Can I have the keys, Dad?"

Charlie gave Jane a look indicating that it was all her fault. "You don't need the keys, son. Just go to sleep."

"Fine."

#25 Reasons

Seth activated the music player on his phone. Loud discotheque beats contrasted sharply against the nocturnal songs of hoot owls and crickets.

"I never thought I'd miss the sound of crickets." Jane muttered to Charlie.

"Hey – at least he won't hear us."

Both Jane's eyebrows went up as his nose and chin tucked down. "Seriously?"

"Why not? Seth's safe in his metal playpen. We're in our private tent. I remember reading something about a 'pleasure-inducing member.' I have one of those. We should try it."

"Well, well." Jane said, allowing herself to be seduced. "If you insist."

"Oh, I do."

"Mom? Dad?"

"What son!" Both parents replied in irritated unison.

"It's raining."

"Oh, for the love of – ice cream!" Charlie amended. "It's just a little rain. You won't melt."

And then the clouds opened.

"Now can I get in the cab?"

"Now you can help me load up." Charlie knew a lost cause when it came raining down like this. "We're going home."

"Seth could just be in the cab. Our tent's waterproof." Jane said. "Mostly."

"We're going HOME."

Thunder punctuated Charlie's decision. The drive home was quiet and soggy.

Phyl Campbell

Don't I have a red cape somewhere? If not, we can improvise.

Lumberjacks and Wolves

Jane grabbed her clock. Bleary eyes barely transmitted the neon numbers to the synapses in her brain. She had to be up in three hours.

"Charlie. You're doing it again."

The resonant sawing of the lumberjack continued.

"Charlie. You're snoring. Roll over or something."

Charlie rolled over to Jane's side. Sleepily, he asked, "You want some of my lovin' baby?"

"If you're awake enough for that, you're awake enough to read to me."

A sleepy Charlie rolled to the other side. A few minutes later, the song of the lumberjack resumed.

Jane shut her eyes. Every woman that ever told her Charlie was a perfect catch needed to get an earful of his midnight symphonies. She trying burying her head with another pillow, but between the actual sound and the vibrations on the bed, it was no use.

Unable to sleep, Jane switched on the light and grabbed the book on her nightstand. *Her Hooded Cloak* was terribly awful, intended as a raunchy romance, but regarded by Jane as comedy. She had brought it to the tent as a joke, knowing there was no way Charlie could take it seriously.

In the story, Red Riding Hood's grandmother tended to all the woodsmen in the forest. She cooked for them and heated up their hearths in other ways as well. When Red reached a "certain age," Granny expected her to take over the family business. Jane knew it was wrong on so many levels, and the part where the Big Bad Wolf climbs into the head woodsman's bed and lies in wait for Red was over the top on all of them. But if she didn't find something to make her laugh, she was going to find an axe and turn lumberjack Charlie into husband stew.

The big bad wolf slinked into the head woodman's cottage. It was empty. She stalked the three sides of the bed that was up against the wall. Then, she gracefully jumped on the bed. She circled three times, then curled up on the bed, happy to have a warm spot to escape the fierce winter winds of the outdoors. If the man came back before Red arrived, she could have dinner as well.

Red Riding Hood approached the first house on Granny's list. In her basket were the ingredients and spices she needed to satisfy each woodsman. She wondered if it would hurt. She knew the mechanics of sex, but the woodsmen always looked so gruff and scary. She could not imagine how Granny had kept them satisfied for so many years. But

46

#25 Reasons

Granny had said she had nothing to worry about; everything she needed was contained in her cloak and in her basket.

"What are you doing up, honey?" Charlie asked sleepily.

"Reading."

"Well, can you do it quieter? When you're turning pages, I can't sleep. And your lamp is awfully bright."

In that moment, Jane imagined Granny Wolf finding the jugular of Charlie Hart. While really too bloody for her taste, it was still quite satisfying. Jane switched off her lamp. She took her book and headed downstairs. Maybe the couch would be a quieter place for reading – or sleeping.

That black one piece.
Yes, that one.
Yes, I am really offering.
No, you cannot skip the reading.
You may take pictures; you may not live to see them. I wouldn't risk it.

Alarm Clock Hell

"Charlie." Jane's voice was quiet, seductive, and half-asleep the next morning. She vaguely remembered coming back up stairs and returning to the bed she shared with Charlie. But here she was.

"Mmmm?"

"Charlie." Jane's voice was less quiet, less seductive, and less than half-asleep. "Charlie, that's your alarm."

"I'll do it at the commercial, honey."

"You're not watching TV, you're sleeping." Jane said, then muttered, "like I'd like to be."

"Five more minutes."

"You're going to be late for work."

"I don't feel good."

"You say that every day."

"I think I'm coming down with something."

"Something else you say every morning. Take some drugs, go see the doctor, or get out of bed and turn off the damn alarm already!" Jane's voice was no longer quiet, seductive, or sleepy-sounding.

Charlie pouted, rolled over, and hit the alarm. It stopped. "You only love me for my paycheck."

49

"Damn straight. Now go earn it and leave me alone."

Jane could never admit to being a model of patience. But she liked to think that if Charlie's alarm woke him instead of her, and she got a full night's sleep instead of being rudely awakened by Charlie's alarm clock thirty minutes before she had to get up to make sure Seth got to school, then she might be more pleasant to him.

Charlie staggered from the bed and into the bathroom. As the bathroom door closed, Charlie's alarm started up again; the combination of buzz and whine promising Jane a killer morning headache.

"Charlie!"

"I must have hit snooze instead of off."

"Make it stop!"

"Sorry, I'll come turn it off in a bit."

"Ugh!" Jane grabbed one of Charlie's pillows and put it over her face. Then she got a solid whiff of it, tossed it back to Charlie's side, and folded one of her own over her exposed ear as she rolled to her side and curled up in the fetal position. She'd do anything, *anything*, to escape the dreaded noise. *Except smell a dirty pillow.* When had she washed sheets last? Something else to add to her unending list. How she'd love to have a job that she left at five. Not that Charlie didn't work hard or provide well. He did both. He even brought work home so he could spend some time with Seth and they could eat dinner together before he put his nose back to the grindstone. It was just hard to appreciate any of those things so early in the morning with something like a fire alarm continuing to emit its blaring tones. "It's so loud! And annoying!"

"I know you are, honey. I still love you."

"I'd kill you, but I'd wind up in alarm clock hell."

The alarm shut off by itself.

"Thank you." Jane said.

"I didn't do it. Must be my lucky day."

"You don't know how good you've got it."

"Yes, dear. Anything you say dear." The alarm clock resumed its auditory torture.

"Argh! Please make it stop!"

Out of the bathroom, Charlie was able to hit the button. "There. It's off now."

"Thank you."

"You know, my side of the bed isn't farther away in the morning than when you're fast asleep in the middle of the night," Charlie suggested. "You could always reach over here and turn it off yourself."

"Can't." Jane insisted. "And I wouldn't encroach at night if you weren't such a covers hog."

"Ah! You've discovered my master plan."

"Did your master plan include a five o clock shadow?"

51

"Naturally."

"Excessive snoring?"

"Of course."

"Halitosis?"

"Cheaper than nitrous oxide and works just as well."

"Not funny."

"Sorry." Charlie leaned in for a morning kiss.

"Ugh – go brush your teeth!"

"I did."

"You did not! Claiming you did is taking a page from Seth's book, for Pete's sake!"

"Now you're just being mean. Pete gets such a bad rap from you."

"I didn't mean your co-worker, Pete. I meant."

"I know. I'm just teasing you. Speaking of Seth, though, isn't it time for him to be getting up?"

"He will when his alarm goes off."

"I'm just going to tell him 'bye.'"

"Don't wake him up, Charlie. And brush your teeth!"

"His alarm will go off in a few minutes anyway."

"Charlie," Jane warned Charlie's retreating figure.

Jane groaned. What was going to happen next was not going to be warm or fuzzy. Would Charlie seriously never learn?

#25 Reasons

"DAD! I hate you!"

"Charlie! I told you!"

"I'm going to work now, since no one in this house loves me."

"Wait – you didn't brush your"

Jane heard the back door open and slam. The garage door opened, and her husband's truck revved. Then she heard tires squeal as the truck drove away.

"Oh, geez. Real mature."

"Mom, Dad gave me a Wet Willy again!"

"I'm sorry, honey. Do you want me to talk to him?"

"No."

"Well, you're up now. Go ahead and get ready for school."

"Dang it."

"No rest for the wicked, honey."

The alarm on Jane's phone chose that moment to start its own morning routine.

"Damn. No rest for the wicked."

Jane swung her feet around and sat up. She let the song play through one chorus before shutting it off. It was time to start the day.

If you read this one to me, we can do it with the lights on – ONCE!

Advice from the Peanut Gallery

"What in the hell are you reading, Charlie?"

Peter was the closest thing Charlie had to a man-friend. They worked together. Sometimes they hung out together. Peter thought he was God's gift to women. Women Charlie knew (including Jane) did not share Peter's inflated opinion of himself.

As Peter swiped the book out of Charlie's hands, Charlie felt he understood why women felt that way. Peter lacked boundaries. "Getting down with some freaky fiction? Charlie, you goat! The shorty on the cover is about to fall all out of that dress! Dang!"

Peter read (Charlie thanked a number of deities that the reading was silent) a few lines and then threw the book down on Charlie's desk. "What the hell kind of garbage crap is that?"

"It's a book." Charlie deadpanned as best he could.

"Wrong. It's not a book." Peter replied with disgust. "This is a girlie book that women give men right after they take their balls and stick them in their purses."

"It's not that bad."

"It's not that bad. It's not that bad. Charlie. Filing your taxes is not that bad. Getting a migraine is not that bad. Tying yourself down to one woman for the rest of your life is not that bad, though why any man would want to be tied down outside of having kinky sex." Peter broke off and shuddered. "Anyway, Charlie. Charlie, listen to me."

"Do I have a choice?"

"Of course you do. But listen, Charlie. Women. They give you books like this and it's all about their needs and sexual purity cycles and meditation and starving children in India and then no sex ever again."

"India has a pretty big population for no one to be having sex there."

"Wrong, Charlie. Wrong." Peter was wound up. "Look. Jane's a great gal."

"I happen to think so."

"No – she is. She's great. But she's going to fill your head with all this romance crap. Then when it comes to the 'freaky chicka bow wow,' our girl Jane's just going to be lying on her back, thinking of England, and making you do all the work."

Charlie would never have admitted it to Peter, but that was how he felt BEFORE reading any of Jane's books. Wasn't he good enough?

#25 Reasons

"What you need, Charlie. What you need. You need some tools, man."

"I have tools, Peter. I have a whole garage full of them."

"Oh, man. Either you're a kinkier freak than I gave you credit for, or you're clueless."

"Let's say I'm clueless."

"Figures." Peter snorted. "Look. There's this store on Eighth and Charles. The chick that works there? She's a real freak. Could give lessons. Maybe she does. Basically, you go there for dinner and she's your floor show."

"Eighth and Charles? You mean For A Good Time Call? That novelty shop where we bought the blow up dolls for Dave's bachelor party?"

"There you go. Yeah. Whatever gets your freak on, man."

"But that's just toys and stuff."

"And stuff. Man, you're killing me!"

"People actually use that stuff? Edible undies and vibrators and"

"You dog. You freaking DOG! You're killing me!"

"Just one problem, Peter. I'm no porn star. And Jane – she'd never go for that. Any of it. So thanks, but."

"Look. I didn't grow up with Jane, but we both went to Southern. Right?"

"Right." Jane had six degrees of separation from nearly anyone in town. Often less.

"And Jane's like a hundred other girls from my high school who want to be the girl next door, right?"

"Right." Charlie wasn't sure he liked where this was going.

"But if you show her you like it, she'll be into it. I swear. You'll have a real freak on your hands, dude."

"OK. Number one. Stop calling me 'dude.' We aren't fourteen. Number two. Find another word besides freak. It's weird."

"C'mon dude," Peter said, emphasizing his blatant disregard for his friend's request. "Don't be so stiff. You want it. She wants it. She just doesn't want to look like a hooker or a slut. But she does want to be a bad girl who gets spanked."

Charlie shook his head. "Why am I getting relationship advice from the single guy again?"

"Because I can embrace my feminine side, my pussy-whipped friend. And because I can get laid by a different girl every week if I want to."

"I hope you use condoms." Charlie said, mostly under his breath.

"I heard that, and I forgive you. Trust me. Go see Hannah at For A Good Time Call. Let her"

#25 Reasons

"I am not going to go see Hannah." Charlie said, cutting Peter off. "I want more sex with my wife. The woman I love. The woman who would shut down your idea of a good time faster than a couple of cops at a teen's kegger when the parents aren't home."

"Well, at least a vibrator and a tickler."

"Stop. We are done with this conversation. So done." Charlie whirled his office chair back around to his computer, but found nothing that needed his immediate attention.

"Oh, now wait a minute." Peter turned his chair back around. "OK. You're a shy gentleman. Or you don't want Jane knowing you were talking to another woman about sex. I can respect that, man. Really."

"Great. Thanks." Charlie started to turn back around.

Peter wasn't finished. "So here's what I'm going to do for you. Hannah gave me this one thing. It's not much. I want a lot more bang for my big buck, ya know, but"

"It isn't used, is it?"

"Aw, hell no! It's still in the wrapper. It's in my desk. Let me get it for you." Peter started to walk away.

Charlie was all for letting him go, but then realized. "Hey, give me back Jane's book!"

"No way, man." Peter called from across the room. "This stuff is poison to dudes. I'm going to disinfect your manhood. And I'll bring you that other file we talked about after lunch."

"Oh, hell." Charlie opened a new browser. His life had gotten easier since the used bookstore put their collection online. He found a replacement copy of Jane's book and placed the order. He could pick it up on his way home and hopefully Jane would be none the wiser.

Still. A part of him was curious. Would Jane like that mysterious thing in the wrapper? Had he been playing it too safe? He wasn't as young as he once was. Maybe a little help wouldn't hurt.

#25 Reasons

Maybe this passage will inspire you to try something new?

Baby it's on... Backwards

"Honey," Charlie called from the bedroom. "I could really use your help in here."

"I can help you, Dad." Seth said.

"No, son!" Charlie barked. "I mean, no – I really need your mother."

"Mom!" Seth yelled down the stairs. "Dad got his junk stuck in his zipper again!"

Charlie would have cheerfully strangled his only son, but that would mean leaving the safety of the bedroom, which he was ill-prepared to do at the moment.

A frazzled Jane appeared at the bottom of the stairs, one hand over the mouthpiece of the phone. "What? We need to leave here in fifteen minutes. Are you about ready?"

"Dad needs you. And all I need is my shoes."

"Well, find them and put them on your feet; we've got to go if we're going to swing by the bank before we meet the Paisleys for dinner. Are you seriously wearing that?"

Jane spoke into phone. "Hey, sweetie, let me call you back tomorrow... I know, I know. Never a dull moment around here, either. Love you, too." She hit "end" on her cell phone as she climbed up the stairs. "Seth, you need to put on a shirt that you didn't spill ketchup on. One with a collar and without an action hero."

Seth grumbled rather loudly, but moved to do what his mother said. He knew better than to argue.

"You know, I think those stairs must have a Jacob's Ladder in there or something." Jane said when she reached the top landing. She stopped to catch her breath before opening the door to her bedroom.

"In here."

Jane shut the door behind her and followed the sound of Charlie's panicked voice to their bathroom. She opened that door, "It always seems like there are more of them anytime I – Charlie, what the hell are you wearing?"

Charlie's cheeks and ear blazed bright red. "Shut the door, please! Seth does not need to see this!"

"We need to be in the car and leaving! We have to go to the bank and then to dinner --"

"Dinner was tomorrow night," Charlie panted – happy to be right and yet still very much in pain.

"Dinner WAS tomorrow night," Jane agreed, "until Stacey remembered Alex's game and asked if we could switch. Since you told me you were coming home early, I just knew it wouldn't be a problem--"

"So now you tell me about the change in plans."

#25 Reasons

"I didn't think I'd need to get you out of, well, what IS that?" Jane grunted while attempting to remove the article from its death grip on her husband's favorite manly bits. "What is this, anyway?"

"I think I managed to put it on backwards, if that's even possible."

"What IS it?" Jane repeated, trying as unsuccessfully to stifle her laughter as she was in getting the thing off her husband.

"Well, you know… In that book you left on my nightstand… There was that one scene you had marked, and, well, you said,"

"I said read it, not reenact it! Gosh, Charlie – you look ridiculous! And I didn't mean that part anyway. You were supposed to read two paragraphs down from there."

"You're the one who placed the sticky note! How was I supposed to know what paragraph?"

"Well, how was I supposed to know you'd pull a stunt like this? We've only been married --"

"You said you wanted to try new things. Spice things up."

"Charlie! We've been married fifteen years. This is not spice! This is salt in a wound!"

"Tell me about it." Charlie winced. He reached out for her, at first Jane thought he wanted to steady himself, but

65

instead her took her hand with one hand and lifted her gaze to his with the other. "Jane – I'm trying. I don't want to lose the best thing that ever happened to me."

Jane was taken aback. Was that a tear in Charlie's eye? The thing must really be hurting him. She tried to move her hands back to help him out of it, but Charlie held her firmly. She could not hold his stare; she had to look away.

"You don't have anything to worry about, Charlie. I'm not going anywhere."

"And I never want you to."

"Ah, screw the bank." Jane said. "Seth?!"

"Yeah, Mom?"

"Call the Paisleys. Tell them your dad got called back into work."

They could hear Seth snort before he called back, "you want me to LIE to your friends?"

"If you do, then you can go ahead and order a pizza for delivery." Downstairs, they heard an undisguised whoop of "YES," which Jane met with, "But only if the Paisleys believe you, Seth, so no funny business."

"Oh, they'll believe me! Dad's got a big project! He told me all about it. And it was boring. So what's really wrong with Dad?"

"He has a tick, OK? And it's engorged."

"A tick? Gross!"

"You wanna see it before I smash it?"

"Uh, no!"

"That's what I thought. Get to calling."

"You handled that very well, wife of mine and mother of the ape-boy. But what if he'd said he wanted to see it?"

"Unlikely, but 'oops, sorry, squished it,' comes to mind." Jane grinned.

"Clever."

"I try. You handle me pretty well too, husband of mine and father of the man-child. He's not getting any younger you know."

"Would you go back to that part where I handle you well?"

"Yeah, sometimes, you do."

"Yeah, well, sometimes, you do, too. In fact, pretty much all the time you do."

"Oh, shut up and kiss me."

Charlie did as he was told – and then some. Then, an odd buzzing sound, like the motor of an electric toothbrush, could be heard over the soft din of lovemaking. Charlie groaned with pleasure first. Jane moaned softly in response. But then the pressure was too much for Charlie.

"Uh, Jane. I think you flipped the switch."

"Uh huh. I tried," Jane said seductively. "Oh, Charlie!"

Phyl Campbell

Charlie could only stand so much intense squeezing pain – made worse by his erection and Jane's enthusiasm – before he just couldn't take it anymore.

"I can't believe I'm doing this, but I need you to stop, Jane." Charlie panted, barely able to force out the words. "It's on, and I really need it not to be on."

"Oh, Charlie." Jane's reaction went from seductive to disappointed to sympathetic in less time than it took an erection to fall flat. She resumed tugging on the device, but it wasn't moving.

"Cut it, Jane. You're going to have to cut it. Please." Charlie was gasping now.

"Cut it?" Jane looked at him, brain not entirely caught up with the conversation.

"Not me! The thing on me. Just cut it off. Carefully."

Jane produced a pair of scissors from the home hair-cutting toolkit.

"OK. Just hold still."

"Please be careful."

"It's not like I've had a lot of experience."

"I know, honey. Just do your best."

"This rubber is really thick."

Charlie wanted to scream at Jane to hurry, but he didn't want her to rush and cut him and he was really in too much pain to do anything more than whimper. The cold steel of the scissor blade and the warmth of Jane's probing hands added another unexpected and not entirely unpleasant element to the operation.

Is this how you pictured we would be in our middle age? I'm just so glad I'm younger than you!

A Very Merry Unbirthday to Jane

Charlie had it all arranged. Seth was spending the night with his grandmother. Dinner had been acquired at that french place Jane loved, the one with the crunchy crusted baguettes and the croque-monsieurs that she said were nothing like ham melts, and not just because they were served on croissants. Everything was set on Jane's best linen tablecloth. He had sent flowers to the school for her, knowing that she wouldn't stay home from her work on the school fundraiser, even on her birthday, and knowing that being able to show the flowers off to other women who understood the appeal of a floral delivery would pay off handsomely toward the end of the evening.

He even had the forethought to buy extra roses and tear off the petals, strewing them about their bedroom in a style reminiscent of that movie she loved. He shoved the leftover stems in the garbage in the kitchen. Nope, he had not missed a detail. Jane was going to have the best thirty-ninth birthday ever.

The best part of his arrangements was in telling Jane (and the teachers) that he had a meeting to attend and was having to miss her special day. The secretary at school had clucked appreciatively at his predicament, at how hard he worked to support his family, and how grateful everyone was to have Jane volunteering for the school fundraisers.

He parked his truck behind the house so any unexpected guests would think they had gone out for the evening. Now he sat on the couch and waited for Jane. School had been out an hour, but if Jane was in the middle of a task she would stay until it was done. He hoped she wouldn't be gone too long--French food didn't reheat well. He looked at the clock on the wall. He had put in a long day. Jane still wasn't home. He snagged a pomme frite from the table. Even French french fries have a half-life, he mused. He swallowed the half he had bitten into and tossed the remainder back on his plate. Hopefully, the sandwich would be enough.

He checked to see that the kitchen was tidy. He realized the thorns were sticking up out of the trash can. Jane wouldn't like that. He lifted them out again and set them on the cutting board. With a large knife, he set about trying to chop the rose stems into more compact pieces. But the stems were unwieldy and the blade did not stay steady. Charlie thought about getting a glove, but with his luck, by the time he found one Jane would be home. It wasn't a big deal. It was just a bunch of stems. Charlie started to hack through the bramble. He tried to find places

72

to hold the stems steady, but kept getting caught on the thorns. Why couldn't rose petals come in strew-able containers – like cupcake liners? Charlie went from gentle chopping motions to more desperate hacking. "What are these stems made of? Lead? Why won't they cut?"

But the partially broken stems continued to ooze and slide away from the knife blade. "I'll show you!"

Charlie got out the cleaver. And in a scene worthy of the Disney *Little Mermaid* Chef, Charlie attacked the stems with the cleaver. And in that same fashion, pulled the cleaver too far back, trying to separate it from the mass of thorny stems, and whacked himself just over his right eye. He swore in pain, then looked to his left and his right to make sure no one had seen what he had done. Fed up with his failure to cut the stems fully, and nicked and scratched in multiple places from the thorns, Charlie snatched the whole mess from the counter and tried to stuff it in the trash can. He left the knife and cleaver in the sink, got an ice pack for his face, wrapped the ice and his hands in towels, and went to sit on the beige-colored couch in the living room. He closed his eyes and set the bag of ice on his face. Much better. He knew he'd hear Jane pull up, and by then surely the bleeding would have stopped and the swelling would go down. Maybe he wouldn't have to tell her about the cleaver. He would rest just for a few minutes.

He wanted to empty the trash so Jane didn't see the thorns. But his head throbbed and the ice felt so nice and cool against it. He'd get up again in a few minutes. He'd take care of everything.

A while later, he was sure he heard Jane's car in the driveway. So he turned on the cd with her favorite music. He didn't care too much for it, but it was her birthday and she should have anything she liked. He surveyed the damage to his hands and head. The towels covering his hands must have slipped when he fell asleep. The bleeding had stopped but there were smears on the couch he'd have to clean up before she walked in. He thoughtfully removed the cushions so Jane wouldn't see the blood, then went to the bathroom to wash the blood off himself and see what his head looked like. He could feel a goose egg rising above his right brow, and his head ached dully. Maybe he had a concussion?

He couldn't imagine what was keeping Jane -- unless she was in the garage on the phone with Amy. He hoped the croquet-monsieur could handle being microwaved once, because there was no way Jane would eat it cold, and it had been hours since he had painstakingly laid it out on the table.

While he was in the bathroom, he heard sirens outside. He vaguely wondered what was going on. He finished washing and changed his shirt. His hands only showed small nicks and scrapes, but his shirt was a huge bloody mess, worse than the couch cushions. The goose egg on his face was a similar purple to Seth's eye just a few short weeks before. His kid could not deny his parentage – that was certain. Charlie was just reentering the kitchen to see Amy pointing a gun at him. She was in uniform, so she must be on duty.

"What the hell, Amy?"

"What are you doing here, Charlie?"

"Uh, I live here?"

Amy swore. "False alarm." She called into the walkie-talkie on her shoulder. "Intruder is visually verified as the husband. He's ok. Though he may not be when his wife gets to him."

"Ten-four." Charlie also heard laughter from the walkie-talkie. He didn't know what was so funny.

Jane ran past Amy and hugged him hard. "Charlie, you're OK, oh, god, there was so much blood. I just knew you were dead. Charlie... Charlie... What the HELL are you doing here Charlie? Sending flowers to school, having Mom pick up Seth, telling everyone you were going away? I come home, your truck's not here, music you hate is playing, knives are in the sink, and you're lying on the

75

couch covered in blood. So either somebody attempted to murder you or you had committed suicide!"

"There wasn't that much blood." Charlie protested weakly.

"I opened the door and you didn't wake up. When I read *Carnal Lust*, they found the wife guilty because she ran up and touched her husband. And if I'd shouted at you while an intruder was still inside the house, I'd have given myself away. So I kept my head. I ran back out to the car in the garage, locked the doors, and called Amy."

"And I spoke to your co-worker," Amy consulted her notes. "Peter said he knew you didn't have a business trip, so we were trying to figure out what 'birthday' was supposed to be code for." Amy added. She obviously wasn't thrilled to have been caught jumping to conclusions like Jane had.

"I come in, see the couch cushions overturned like someone's looking for valuables, and I think maybe Jane isn't just overreacting. But what was all the birthday stuff about?"

"It's Jane's thirty-ninth birthday. I wanted to do something special for her."

"It's not her birthday." Amy said.

"Thirty-nine!" Jane cried at the same time.

"October tenth. It's your birthday. Ten ten."

#25 Reasons

"My birthday is the sixteenth, you idiot. Last year you told Seth it would be great if it was the tenth, and then you just confused yourself. And I won't be thirty-nine."

"Oh, I know, honey. Wink wink."

"No really."

"Uh huh. Just keep telling yourself that."

"Charlie." Amy said.

"Yeah, Amy? I mean Officer, I guess, since you're on duty."

"Jane's my age."

"I know. I know. She keeps saying she's younger and then she confuses herself."

"I'm thirty-eight."

"Oh."

"But I must say this table is laid out beautifully. Where's this take out from? Dionne's?"

"Le Maurice's. It's her favorite."

Amy picked up a fry and sampled it. "Damn. Gourmet fries have a shelf life shorter than Micky D's."

"Tell me about it." Charlie complained.

"Still, it's the thought that counts, Jane. Don't be too hard on him. I've got to be getting back to the station. Can you two handle it from here?"

"Of course, Amy. So sorry we bothered you." Jane purred. She hated to be embarrassed, which Charlie thought a shame since she blushed so prettily when she was.

"No bother. Just doing my job, ma'am," Amy drawled with a chuckle.

"Good night, Amy."

"Good night, Amy."

Jane closed the door behind her friend. Then she walked over to the table and picked up the sandwich on the plate which she knew was meant for her. "Croque-monsieur. You remembered."

"Of course I remembered. You only talk about it all the time."

"Think you'll remember it next week when it really is my birthday?"

"Absolutely."

"Liar."

"You're probably right..."

Charlie paused, then decided to go for broke.

"Well, since it's not your birthday, and I did send you flowers, do you think"

"Don't even think about it. You thought I was thirty-nine."

"I was close. Besides, babe, age is nothing but a number..."

#25 Reasons

Jane carried both plates over to the kitchen trash. She looked pointedly at him, but did not comment. Instead, she asked, "are you gonna eat this?"

"No."

"Me neither."

"Pizza?"

"Sounds good."

"Little Italiano's?"

"Do they deliver?"

"I think so."

"Even better. We've got to get this blood off the couch cushions so Seth doesn't freak out tomorrow and I'm starving."

Charlie went to call. He had just heard Joe call out "Little Italiano's: home of the pizza Marguerite" when he heard Jane yell, "Son of a bitch!"

"Sorry, gotta call you back," Charlie said quickly. He ran back to the kitchen and to Jane.

Jane's hands were dripping blood all over the white trash bag and into the garbage can.

"Oh, shit." Charlie said. "The thorns."

"Yeah, the thorns."

"Oh, baby. Here, let me help you."

"Charlie?"

"Yeah, Jane?"

"This birthday sucks." Jane tried to laugh, but tears fell instead.

"It's not your birthday."

"Now you remember."

"I'll do better next week."

"Promise?"

"Promise."

Read this passage and do what it says. I'll pretend I'm her. What have you got to lose?

The Gift of Dance

"He bought me the idea of dance lessons." Jane said
by way of greeting. Then she and Amy hugged carefully –
to avoid spilling the drinks Amy held -- and sat down at the
outside table of the coffee shop. The October mornings
were a bit cool now, but not glacial like they'd be from
Halloween to the end of Spring Break. They were going to
enjoy them for as long as they could.

"Here. Happy Birthday." Amy said, passing Jane a hot
chocolate before flipping the lid back on her cappuccino.
"Did I hear you right? Charlie bought you dance lessons?'

"Almost. Buy is the wrong word. But he sent this to
my email this morning. I'm sure he thinks it will make up
for the other night."

Amy accepted Jane's phone and read the email out
loud. "'Good for six lessons at your choice of ballroom or
modern dance studio.' Jane, that's awesome! Why aren't
you thrilled?"

"One. It's not even a gift card. He made a Word Doc
or a Power Point or something without actually making any
sort of commitment. He has no intention of making that

commitment. Two. Charlie would rather break his leg – make that both legs – than go dancing with me. Three."

"Aren't you being a little over the top?"

"Charlie didn't dance with me at our own wedding. And never while we were dating – I do not count the ten second sophomore shuffle in the kitchen, either. Especially not when I'm in the middle of burning breakfast."

"He did buy you dinner from Le Maurice's or wherever. And it's obvious he felt bad about how things played out the other night. Couldn't he have had a change of heart about the dancing?"

"Change? Charlie? Those two C words do not belong in the same sentence. Charlie does not change, and he does not have good ideas. For my thirty-fifth birthday, for example, he bought me a SUGAR FREE cake."

"And he's still alive?"

"I look terrible in prison orange."

"But still, that's not the same guy who bought you roses."

"And left the thorny stems unwrapped and in the trash."

Amy did a double-take at Jane's palms, still scratched from the encounter. "Oh, dear."

#25 Reasons

"It doesn't even matter, because number three is the worst of them all. The absolute clincher for why this idea of dance lessons will never – ever – happen."

"I can't even begin to guess."

"Ricky Florida."

"Oh, hell. That's a name I haven't heard in forever."

"You don't get out, much, officer." Jane grinned.

"I get out plenty."

"I mean when you're not answering domestic disturbances or arresting people."

"A woman's got to sleep sometime."

"Here." Jane finished fiddling with her phone and handed it to Amy. "Press play."

"What's this?" Jane asked, accepting the phone. Then her eyes got big. "Oh, Jane. Ooh la la. Who is THAT dreamboat?"

"Amy, meet the new and improved Ricky Florida."

"No." Amy gasped and nearly dropped Jane's phone.

"Yes." Jane's face was scrunched up like she was touring an empty and smelly men's locker room. "I've been to his website. Read his bio. One hundred percent sure he's the same guy."

"Isn't he the one that got on the cafeteria table and sang that song for you in front of everybody?"

"That's Ricky. It was a long time ago, though."

"Jane. You threw your lunch at him and told him to take a cold shower!"

"He was embarrassing me!"

"It was sweet. Kind of."

"We were in seventh grade and he was dressed like a minstrel."

"Yeah. Explaining your reaction to the costuming lady in the drama department probably wasn't fun for him."

"What did he care? He was holding hands with another girl a week later."

"Can't bring yourself to say her name can you?"

"Nope. She ran off and started holding hands with Mason Jefferson a week after that. Tramp. Broke poor little Ricky's heart. I didn't want any boyfriend. But she was mean."

"Ah. Tween-age drama. Having to deal with any of that with Seth yet?"

"Thankfully no. He's like both his parents. He likes girls, but they're just boys who wear dresses on occasion. We may skip cooties and dating all together. And every time he tells me that a friend has a girlfriend, we go out and I buy him a new video game. Much cheaper than being a grandparent."

"So the fight at school wasn't about a girl?"

#25 Reasons

"The fight, if you could call it that, wasn't anything more than Seth trying to keep a bully in line. Not succeeding. But trying."

"Really takes after Charlie, huh?" Amy snickered.

"Watch it. I'm still good at throwing my lunch."

Amy threw her arms up, indicating surrender. "But back to Ricky. Surely he's not the only dance teacher out there. Lots of us took dance. Where are all those teachers?"

"Ricky is the only couples' teacher for modern or ballroom. And most of the teachers we had are arthritic and retired. Ah, the benefits of being a grown up in the same place where I grew up."

"Crap. Does Charlie know?"

"Know what? That when I was in seventh grade I dumped my lunch tray on a guy because he was singing to me and looked better in tights than I did? That he may or may not remember that? That he may or may not hold a grudge?"

"Any and all. You were seventh graders. That was a long time ago."

"You remembered."

"It was epic!"

"You're not helping."

"Anyway, Ricky looks good in this video. How long ago was this?"

"Last month."

"What the hell?"

"I know. He looks great."

"Well, so do you," Amy was almost too quick in her defense.

"I look my age," Jane sighed. "Ricky looks like them." She pointed across the way to two young college girls drinking coffee and taking selfies.

"Well, they look ridiculous. They should be in class or something. You know you look good for your age. Charlie was just being Charlie. Don't let him get you down. He didn't mean to insult you."

"At least he's still older than me."

"True."

"And I don't let him forget it."

"Good girl."

"Anyway, Charlie thinks he can earn points with me just by offering dance lessons. That I will say it's the thought that counts and that I never expected him to actually go because he's perfect the way he is."

"And what if Charlie really wants to give you dance lessons?"

"A sugar free cake is not a cake," Jane replied, as if that explained everything, "even though the word "cake" is in there. Ricky Florida may have sugar free cake for his birthday. That's not what I want for mine. Any more than I want dance classes taught by a man who used to have a thing for me with my husband who will not want to be there and who will complain the entire time."

"Look – why don't you tell Charlie you love the gesture but you don't want the dance lessons?"

"And let him off the hook? What kind of message would that send him?"

"That maturity becomes you in your old age."

"Not fair. Not funny."

"Tell Charlie your single friend needs dance lessons and Ricky Florida's home phone number."

"Ricky's mom's still alive. I'm sure we could call her up. She'd be thrilled to talk to us again. Remember she was always saying what cute little girls we were?"

"We were pretty cute. And she made awesome churros for us. But no, I'm not getting set up by RICKY FLORIDA'S MOTHER." Amy gulped down the last swig of coffee. "Ugh. I hate it when the dregs get cold. So anyway -- what are you going to tell Charlie?"

"I don't know."

"What would one of your heroines do?"

"I can't think of a single hero/heroine situation where the two principles didn't know how to dance."

Phyl Campbell

"Maybe show is a better word. Maybe I'll just show him this video. I mean, just the costume"

"You don't see Charlie as El Matador?" Amy giggled.

Jane laughed, too. "Run screaming for the hills, he will."

"And then he'll still owe you."

"I should think so. And I'm not planning on letting him off the hook anytime soon."

"Good idea. You shouldn't. In the meantime, let me see your phone again? I want to get Ricky's number."

Read this passage about America's favorite pastime and I'll ride you like a cowgirl.

Sexual Congress

"Ugh!" Jane typed angrily at her laptop, alternating between furious typing and sitting back, scowling, while her eyes scanned the page.

"What's the matter?" Charlie asked – as if he didn't know. He'd been hearing the sound bites for over an hour while Jane sat and seethed. Charlie didn't know what Jane was worried about. She was married – to him. He accepted her as she was. No politician was going to make laws that regulated her body. But Jane was hell bent on saving the world -- or at least muckraking the heck out of it.

Jane didn't notice Charlie's facetiousness. "Oh – these stupid morons! They still haven't figured out that the world should not be responsible for zipping their pants for them." Jane returned to furious typing.

"Are you stirring the pot again, sweetheart?" Charlie grinned. His idea of reading about sex and Congress was probably limited to Tom Clancy or James Patterson. Jane recently discovered Catherine Coulter – any of which would be preferred to the urbane romances. And fiction was always better than Jane getting so worked up over reality.

"Well, they just get so stuck on themselves. Look at this guy."

Charlie got off the couch and walked over to Jane's desk. He looked at her laptop over her shoulder.

"Who's stuck on himself?" He asked -- though he already knew. He liked it when she was riled up.

"These damn politicos! No contraception, no abortion, no gay marriage."

"No lives. No fun. Stupid pricks," Charlie agreed.

"And these stupid people who think everything that comes out of their mouth is God's own truth when they KNOW better. They should know better! This guy -- he should know better!" Jane sat back, waiting for her comment to post and reading other responses. "'Women should stay home and raise babies.'" She quoted the poster. "Is he a moron or an idiot?"

"Are they mutually exclusive?" Charlie asked aloud. But Jane wasn't paying attention.

"As if." She replied aloud to the words on the screen. "Where would the senator's whore come from if women didn't enter the workplace?" She typed as she talked.

"They're called interns," Charlie offered as he watched her fingers fly over the keys. He noticed that sometimes the words she typed matched what she said. Other times they didn't. He didn't know how she did that. He couldn't type when someone was talking to him. She was talking to him, to herself, and to the nameless idiot on social media – without seeming to miss a keystroke. He continued, "Unless the senator orders a stripper or a call girl or something. Then they are called that."

"It's called disgusting. And hypocritical. And demeaning to women."

"Your blue streak is showing, dear." Charlie suppressed a grin. "I didn't know I married a liberal."

"It's not a Democrat thing. They're no better than the Republicans. It's a woman thing, and it's an equality thing. A fairness thing." Jane finished typing turned around to face him. Her arms were crossed in a way that told Charlie she was up to being distracted a bit. He could do that. And he didn't need some romance novel's help, either.

"Would that be a pink thing? Maybe a lacy pink thing?" He suggested without a hint of subtlety.

"Do I own anything pink or lacy?" Jane asked. Her arms were still crossed over her chest.

Charlie knew he had to play this carefully, lest Jane go from "up for distraction" to "too pissed off to be distracted." It was a close-run thing.

"OK. You've got a point." Charlie said agreeably. "So it's a black, silky thing?"

Phyl Campbell

"Yes, honey." Jane snorted, turning back to her laptop. "My politics are a black silky thing."

She wasn't getting away that fast. Charlie pressed his advantage.

"Oh, baby. Sign me up for some sexual congress." He stood behind Jane, his chin on top of her head in a way he knew she hated but couldn't ignore. She whirled her chair around again in response.

"Charlie! I'm being serious! Women everywhere are…"

"Not part of my sexual congress." He was ready for her. By turning around, Charlie caught Jane's legs and pulled her up to him for a kiss. "Only you are."

"Oh, Charlie. It's a good thing I like you." Jane said as she kissed him playfully.

"Hey, what's not to like?" Charlie said. "I'm both fixed and housebroken. All that's left is for you to feed and pet me."

"Charlie!" Jane swatted at him as he led her to the bedroom. Sexual congress, indeed.

Read this to me and I promise I won't fall asleep before you're done.

Early to Bed, Early to Rise

"It says, 'He looked deep into her amber eyes and said "I want to watch you when I do this to you."'" So you have to keep your eyes open for this, Jane." Charlie protested.

"I don't have to. Just because it's in the book, that doesn't mean we have to do it exactly that way," Jane panted. They were both naked, in bed, and Jane was under Charlie. Charlie was mostly keeping his weight on one arm, but he was holding her book with the other and pressed his weight on her when turning the pages. She was past beginning to think this was a really bad idea.

"Hey, this was your idea. I just think if we're doing it, we should do it right. No fair closing your eyes and pretending I'm somebody else."

Charlie shifted his weight again, which caused Jane first to groan, then to yelp. Jane couldn't tell whether or not he was doing it on purpose or in an attempt to be funny.

"Hey -- watch those knees! I can't get out of your way when you're on top of me."

"This would be a whole lot easier if we were younger."

"No kidding."

"And in better shape."

"Ugh! Don't remind me."

"Hey -- at least you get time to work out."

"You didn't birth a baby."

"When is that excuse going to get old?"

"When it stops being true -- hey -- watch it!"

"I can't help it. I'm old and decrepit." Charlie faked a wheeze, and then fake-fainted, putting all his weight on Jane.

In response, Jane tried to shove Charlie into a position that would cause her less pain and allow her to actually breathe.

"No, no, no!" Charlie insisted. Propping himself up again. "You're not supposed to do that. I web-searched this. You're supposed to have one leg up here like so," Charlie moved Jane's leg into what Jane considered an inhumane position, "and then --"

"Ow! Charlie -- my leg does not go that way naturally! Charlie! Stop it!"

"Fine." Charlie accepted Jane's shoving and rolled off her completely.

"You don't have to go all the way away. We could just cuddle for a bit or something." Jane suggested.

#25 Reasons

"You say that. Then I'm going to come over there and nature will take its course and then you're going to get mad."

"Well, then you lay on your back and I'll spoon you from the side."

"Yay." Charlie dead-panned. "I can't wait." But he lay on his back anyway, and Jane sidled up next to him. She ran her fingers up and down his belly.

"Hey, if I can't play like that, why can you?" He asked.

"Because you like it when I break the rules." Jane said. "Besides, when you do it, it tickles. And not in a sexy way."

"My tickling is not sexy?" Charlie fake-pouted. This was familiar territory.

"Not at all." Jane smirked, never ending the movement of her fingers as they played from belly to chest and back again. For added benefit, she blew softly across his earlobe. He shivered, and not from cold.

"Do I do anything that's sexy?" Charlie asked.

"Well, sometimes you only snore lightly."

"My snoring is sexy?"

"Only the light snoring. The lumberjack snoring does nothing for me." Jane continued to breathe the words into Charlie's ear. She enjoyed the effect she still had on him.

Charlie closed his eyes and pretended to demonstrate the lumberjack snoring. He wanted sex with her, but he also wanted her to work for it for a change – to throw her off her game.

"Yep. That definitely does not get my motor running." She breathed. She knew what he was doing, but these were games she always won. And for good reason.

In his fake sleep, Charlie rolled back on top of Jane, continuing to snore loudly.

"Ugh! Get off! Stay on your side." If he was going to play rough, she would take her body and leave.

"Need my lovey." Charlie pretended to talk in his sleep.

Jane elbowed him hard. "Get your own lovey."

Charlie opened his eyes. "I did get my own lovey. I married my lovey." He propped up on one elbow and hovered over Jane the way he'd seen many hunks do in movies.

"Oh, Charlie. You say such sweet things."

"I love you, Jane." He kissed her softly.

"I love you, too, Charlie." She kissed him back.

They were quiet for a minute, staring into each other's eyes, just long enough for something to happen that made Jane break the silence.

"Charlie!"

"What?"

#25 Reasons

"You're ready to go again? I thought we were just kissing."

"What can I say? I've got my lovey and I'm happy."

"'Lovey?' Is that a technical term?" Jane asked.

"Yes."

"Are you sure about that?"

"As sure as I need to be. Come here, Lovey." Charlie pulled Jane close to him. She didn't protest.

"Let's see what your silly romance novel has to say about this move..."

"Charlie!"

Leather and Lace –

How 'bout I zip on my boots and wear that black lace one you like so much?

Are You Coming With Me Or Not?

"I need milk and soda from the store before everything gets crazy." Jane told Charlie while putting on her coat. Thanksgiving was two days away, and the stores were already insane.

"Let me go with you." Charlie offered.

"Just tell me what you need."

"I don't know yet. I will when I get there."

"Really? You don't know if you're out of something?"

"No. I'm hungry for something. I just don't know what."

"Babe. I'm running in. I'm getting two things. One or two more things wouldn't make that much difference. But I don't want to saunter up and down every aisle of the store where people are already going holiday nuts while you try to decide if you want something."

"Just go then. I'll go later if I still want something."

"Now that's pretty ridiculous. I'm already going. Right now. Just tell me what I can get for you."

"All right. Why don't you get some of those microwave dinners – the big ones – but with the Salisbury steak, not the meatloaf this time? And then maybe some baby carrots. Yeah, those would be good. And nacho cheese dip – the kind that isn't mild, but isn't too spicy? And I'll want chips to go with that. Maybe a veggie tray. Yeah. I'm feeling like a veggie tray."

"Charlie. That's five things. Five very specific things. Why don't you put those on a list?"

"Then don't worry about it. I'll just go later."

"Put your shoes and coat on and come with me now. Let's just do this."

"Fine. We'll take my truck."

"Really? Groceries will fit better in the car."

"You said you only had two things."

"And then you rattled off a list! And one thing will lead to another – it always does."

"Didn't you just go to the store yesterday?"

"I did, but the milk dates weren't very far out, and I wanted to have more soda since you and Seth will both be home for the holiday weekend."

"So we're out of milk."

"No – it expires tomorrow."

"So why don't you just go tomorrow?"

"Because I'm putting on my coat NOW and I have time NOW and it seemed like a good idea. Are you coming with me or not?"

"Yeah. I don't get why you keep buying soda, though. You keep saying you need to cut back."

"Yes," Jane seethed. "But then I have conversations like this one and soda's cheaper than alcohol."

"What do you mean?"

"Never mind. We will take the truck. I will get milk and soda. While I'm doing that, you can get whatever you want. I'll meet you at the registers."

"Well, now you're taking all the fun out of it."

"Fun? Grocery shopping isn't fun."

"Depends on the company."

"Fine. Grocery shopping is not fun – with you."

"Why not?" Charlie asked.

"Seriously?"

"I'm fun."

"Debatable at the moment."

"No, really. I'm fun!"

"Can we just go? I've only got a little bit left in my book and I'd like to finish it tonight."

"Why don't you finish your book now and then we'll all go later."

"Because when I finish my book, I want to be in my bed and comfortable. I have my shoes on now. My coat is on now. I'm psyched to go now so when I'm reading my book, I'm not thinking about the errand that I already ran."

Phyl Campbell

"So send Seth. He has a bike. Read your book and send Seth to the store."

"No thank you. I would not want Seth carrying milk and soda in the basket of his bike."

"Why not? I used to."

"And you walked uphill ten miles to school and home."

"In the snow."

"Not the desert?"

"Oh. Yeah, right. The desert. It was so hot. There was no water for miles."

"So how could you walk ten miles uphill both ways if you had a bike?" Seth didn't even look up from the video game.

Charlie was flummoxed. "Uh, well, we, uh – we weren't allowed to have our bikes at school."

"Lame."

"I know, right?"

"Yeah. You're lame."

"Hey." Charlie protested.

"Focus!" Jane snapped.

Charlie and Seth both faced her, sheepish looks on their faces.

"That's better. Now. Last chance. Are you coming?

Charlie chuckled.

"What?"

110

#25 Reasons

"Did you hear yourself?"

"I just asked if you were – oh. I see. Real mature."

Charlie about fell over laughing.

"Oh, yes. I'm a comedy giant. Here all week. I'm going."

"Wait! Don't go without me!"

As Jane closed the door that led to the garage, Charlie struggled to get out of his chair and slip some shoes on.

"Wait! Wait!"

Jane stopped the car halfway down the driveway. Charlie opened the passenger door and got in.

Jane was still thinking she should have flown solo, and they hadn't left the driveway. She sighed heavily.

"What's the matter?" Charlie asked.

If you can read this whole passage and NOT LAUGH, then yes, I will let you try the whipped cream thing.

Ignoring the Elephant

"I still don't understand why we have to go to this thing."

"Your boss expects you to make an appearance with your lovely wife. Maybe when you show up with me, he'll let you leave early. Besides, Rachel just had her baby and I haven't seen Deirdre since" Jane stopped mid-sentence. "Oh, wait."

Charlie came to Jane in the closet of their bedroom, fighting with his holiday tie. "Wait, what? Did you change your mind? We could order pizza and watch a movie. I'll even let you pick the movie."

"No. I forgot I won't see Deirdre at the party this year."

"Oh, yeah. I guess that's right. She and Kevin split up."

"Ugh! Why do so many people separate right before the holidays?"

"Right before the holidays? We knew just after school started."

"True. I just got caught up in other stuff and forgot about it, I guess."

"Tell you what. Why don't you call her and catch up? I'll be downstairs, minus this noose, watching the game."

"Charlie! We can't not go. I just need to remember to call Deirdre next week."

"And say what?"

"And say I'm thinking about her and I hope she'd handling everything OK."

"And if she's not?"

"I don't know. I'll listen. Offer moral support."

"You're not bosom buddies, though. She doesn't have kids at Seth's school. You haven't run into her at the store. Do you even have her phone number?"

"I'll get it from Kevin tonight."

"Yeah, because that won't be awkward."

"No, it'll be fine. I'll just tell Kevin I need to call her because"

"No, Jane. It would be awkward. You don't need to call her. You were the spouses of co-workers who saw each other at holiday parties and company picnics. Outside that? You two never talked."

"Isn't that sad?"

"Isn't what sad?"

"The work spouses. She probably feels awkward talking to any of us. We feel awkward reaching out to her, I don't know anything about why they're not together anymore – whether she's happy or miserable or if there was cheating and who or why."

"Which one's the transplant?"

"Transplant?"

"You know. Your family is from here. You graduated from here. I'm the transplant. I didn't grow up here."

"Oh. I get it. Transplant. Cute." Jane thought for a minute. "I don't think either of them are natives. But they're both older than me by quite a bit, so maybe they're both natives and our paths just hadn't crossed before. I mean, I don't know everybody."

"Are you sure? I thought you did."

Jane ignored that. "Maybe I can just ask Rachel at the party tonight."

"You just have to stir the pot, don't you?"

"What do you mean?"

"We're going to this holiday office party to amuse my boss. You're going there to talk to people you haven't talked to since the last work function that spouses attended, and you're plotting to return tonight to get dirt on somebody who no longer has any ties to you?"

"When you put it that way, it sounds silly."

"It is silly. It's ridiculous."

"OK. Then I'll try my best to be like everyone else and ignore the elephant in the room."

Phyl Campbell

"That's all I'm asking."

Something was gnawing at Jane. She had lots of
Deidres in her life. Amy was great, but she was single and
didn't understand that marriage was no picnic. Plus, she
worked all the time. Seth's friends' moms all worked. Some
admitted they were envious of her – of her freedom. Jane
was envious of them – of theirs. The stay at home moms
she visited were always trying to sell her something – make
up or jewelry or a new way to polish her nails. She needed
someone who wasn't in the thick of the rat race.

She had thought Deidre was going to be that. Deidre
and Kevin had met on a single's cruise. Both were older.
Both had been married before. Deidre had a kid from her
previous marriage, but he was grown. Jane wondered what
caused the split. Both seemed like level-headed people, and
she had really been looking forward to getting to know
Deidre better.

She felt like she'd lost something. Something she
didn't quite have in the first place. Still, Charlie was right.
She should ignore the elephant in the room and not cause
trouble.

Kevin's home was festive enough, meaning that either
he had a flair for decorating Jane did not associate with him

116

or he hired a service to complete the task. Jane wondered for the umpteenth time how much a service like that cost, and whether they put up your décor or brought in their own. There were no pictures of Deidre anywhere like there were last year.

"Thanks for coming, everyone." Kevin was saying. Then he went on to talk about sales numbers and projections and stocks – Jane tuned him out. She smiled at Rachel and waved. When Kevin quit flapping his jaw, she'd walk across the room and hold that baby. She had absolutely no desire to be pregnant or the mother of an infant again, but there was something so soothing about new baby smell.

Was Charlie satisfied just having the one? She knew he'd wanted more kids. In just about every romance with kids that Jane had read, there were usually a pair. Often a boy and a girl, but sometimes a pair of boys. More often, the protagonists had pets – dogs or cats. Jane could not imagine adding a dog to the relative human chaos of her home. And Charlie absolutely hated cats. So they told Seth early on to make friends with as many pet owners as possible. Seth used to come home talking about how the siblings would fight over whose turn it was to walk the dog, so he'd do it. He didn't understand what the big deal was. Jane imagined him living on a farm with a ton of pets.

She shook her head. No sense imagining him any more grown up than he already was. She turned her attention back to the décor.

Kevin had good taste. Strong gray stone adorned the fireplace mantel. The hardwood floors gleamed with fresh polish, yet Jane hadn't noticed anyone slipping. Her own conservative heels were quiet on the hardwood – a clear sign of a good foundation underneath. Charlie would know what kind of wood it was. If she wanted to hear the whole history of wood flooring, she'd consider asking him. Instead, she'd remain curious.

The carpet in her home was a bit outdated, but so much easier with Seth in the house. Jane remembered when Seth was just learning to walk and she had yoga mats everywhere. Did she still have them in the attic now? Maybe she should offer them to Rachel.

Charlie squeezed her shoulder. "You're doing it again," he whispered.

He couldn't read her mind, she thought. "Doing what?" She whispered back.

"Overthinking."

"How would you know?"

"Your eyes are open."

"Oh. Ha Ha."

#25 Reasons

But he was right again. The mats had been up in the attic for years. Rachel's baby wasn't even close to crawling yet, much less walking.

"This is the part where the two lovers see each other across the room for the first time."

"What?"

"In your books. In the young adult novels, the teacher is droning on and on, but in adult books, it's a boss, or a client, or a customer – someone who thinks they are important but are totally irrelevant to the story."

"What a brilliant observation, Charlie."

"Not so different from your books."

"Maybe." Jane agreed.

"I say we take a page out of one of our books and get out of here."

"We just got here."

"Yeah, and so now we can leave. Great plan. I'll get the car."

"Charlie. I haven't said 'hello' to Rachel yet. I'm not leaving."

"Fine. Just promise me no elephants."

"I won't embarrass you."

"Not good enough. Promise – no elephants."

"Fine. I promise. No elephants."

Kevin's remarks drew to a close as everyone toasted cheers with raised glasses. Jane went over to Rachel, hands out to hold the baby. She babbled and made faces and talked new mom-stuff with Rachel while Charlie made his professional hobnobbing rounds.

It was good to see Rachel. It was good to play with the baby. But these weren't her friends. She didn't like avoiding Peter but she still couldn't look at him after the whole sex-toy incident. She also had a feeling he was partially responsible for the birthday mishap.

One hour passed, and then another. Jane was exhausted from not mentioning the elephant in the room. When Charlie suggested they leave third time, she nearly ran to the car.

Maybe after reading this, you'll get why I was laughing at dinner the other night. What am I saying – I have no idea when you'll find this one.

Hard for the Money

After the winter break, Jane's sticky note list looked something like this:

Confirm bands
Confirm authors
Confirm artists
Confirm layout
Run by W, DG, S

Charlie had long since given up trying to figure out what it all meant. Authors, that made sense, but who brought artists and bands to a used book sale? And what was W, DG, S?

Jane was excited, though, more excited than he'd seen her since stirring the pot in college. Hell, she was sexy when she was on a steamroll.

"You're going to bring Seth to school this afternoon, right?"

"School on Saturday?" Charlie grinned.

"You're joking, right? Anyway, I need to be there at noon, and I'd rather not have him bored or have to come

123

Phyl Campbell

back to get him." Jane was putting her coat on as she talked, and gathering her purse and list.

"Yes, I'm joking. I know the fundraiser is today. You've only told me to 'keep the last Saturday in January clear' since what – October something? And if we're not making Seth walk, I guess I can be his ride." Then Charlie smirked, "what's in it for me?"

"My undying affection, Charlie. My undying affection."

"I bet you say that to all the boys."

Jane rolled her eyes. "You may want to leave that and other great lines to Meatloaf."

"Meatloaf? Is that what we're having for dinner tonight?" Seth interrupted as he entered the room and therefore the conversation.

"I'm surrounded by hooligans." Jane protested. "No, Seth. Dinner is pizza at the school. You'll probably want to get there between three thirty and four. Do you have your armband and your dad's?"

"Yeah, Mom. I got 'em."

"Good." Jane paused. "Show me."

Seth reached into his first pocket and came up empty-handed Back pockets, no armbands. Jane was starting to lose patience when he said "wait a minute" and reached into the cargo pocket. "BINGO!" he said, revealing the

124

paper strips that would give him and his father access to the event.

"Hey!" Charlie protested. "How come you trust Seth -- and not me -- with those?"

"Because I can ground him." She replied. Then she turned back to Seth. "Great. Don't lose them. Not only do they get you in everywhere, they identify you as being with fundraiser staff so you can get to me if you need to."

"We won't need to."

"Yeah, we'll be fine."

"I'm counting on it."

When four o clock rolled around, Charlie found himself staring at a field of cars. "No wonder your mom didn't want to leave and come back. I bet she got a primo parking place."

Seth just grinned.

The two had about decided to return home in the truck and come back on foot, but finally Seth spotted a grassy spot where the truck would fit.

"Are all these cars here because of Mom?"

"Looks like it."

"What all is she doing?"

"I have no idea. Let's go check it out, shall we?"

Phyl Campbell

They trekked across the school grounds and finally made their way to the front door. With their armbands, they weren't subjected to the line of people waiting outside to get in.

"Are all these people here to trade books?" Seth asked incredulously.

"Mr. Hart. Seth. So glad you could make it." Seth recognized the new assistant librarian. "Jane got tied up, but wanted me to make sure you didn't have any problems getting in. We're just so grateful for everything she was able to get together. This kind of response just blows me away. Would you like a tour?" Without pausing for more than a second, the woman guided Charlie and Seth toward the first hallway.

"Jane was quite the ingénue," she said. You know how she divided the school's hallways into dedicated genres, got vendors to bid for booth space, then got local bands to bid for performance space?"

Charlie had heard something about that, but didn't know.

"Anyway, this is the children's wing. Kid Power Rocks has the last classroom at the end of the hall. Books line the hall walls, and the other classrooms have art sales, classes,

126

author or fan readings and of course local author book booths. Oh, here's a map of everything." She handed them school maps reworked with the various vendors and performing groups. It reminded Charlie of a huge fair – if fairs were ever held indoors.

"Every vendor paid over a hundred dollars to be here, and Jane had a waiting list in case any of them canceled or didn't pay on time. October was fierce. We were so swamped with calls and emails. But Jane had her system – all those little sticky notes kept us on track."

"That I can believe," laughed Charlie.

"Seth, you can help your dad with some of this. Western stuff is in the history hall, with Long Dirt Road playing at the end. Sci Fi is in the science wing with that Indie Band, Devil's" she paused, trying to think of the name, "something."

"Devil's Due is playing here? Today?"

"Devil's Due. Thanks, Seth. That's the one."

"Wow!" Too late, Seth tried to curb his enthusiasm. "I mean, that's kinda cool."

"Do you like that band, Seth?" Charlie had never heard of them.

Seth rolled his eyes at his father. Their guide was sympathetic to Charlie. "I'd never heard their music, but they're apparently really popular with this age group."

127

Phyl Campbell

"Duh." Seth said.

"Anyway, classics are in the foreign language hall."

"Who's the band for classics?" Charlie wanted to know.

"There's a string quartet that won the spot. Six hundred dollars to come and play, but they're also selling CDs and handing out information about their music school. We have many band members advertising some kind of music lessons. And artists offering art lessons. I had no idea how much talent we had in our community!"

"Six hundred dollars? To play in a classroom?" Seth was stunned. "They paid Mom that?"

"They paid the school that, but your mother is the one who convinced them to."

"Darn. Mom could have been rich. Right Dad?"

"Yeah, son." Charlie was thinking about how much money party planners made per hour. Did Jane want a career doing this? It would certainly look great on her resume. "Six hundred dollars, you said?"

"Groups applied for spaces with sealed bids. And they could check a box if they wanted the room to themselves or didn't mind sharing. Like sometimes two performers would share a space so they could perform in sets with breaks between. Jane worked all that out."

"So what's in the library?" Charlie joked.

"Actually, that's the new PTA central. There were too many books in there that couldn't wander off, and the central location made it good for Jane to be able to collect money and reach the office."

"I guess that makes sense." Charlie said. This event was huge. Books were everywhere. Jane's typical sticky notes had been replaced by large printer labels identifying shelves by genre and indicating the first letter of the author's last name.

"To be honest, we thought Jane was crazy when she said she was going to buy book cases to line the walls instead of using cafeteria tables. But look at this. I mean just look."

"So how much has Mom raised so far?"

"Well, we won't know actual numbers until Monday, but just on vendors bidding for spaces, she netted the school twenty thousand dollars."

Seth's chin dropped. "Mom did that?"

"Don't act so surprised, Seth. Your mom is awesome." Charlie said, though he was having a hard time believing it himself. "But seriously – how did the vendors afford that?"

"Oh, they could raise money or be sponsored. We have quite a few students whose parents or teachers sponsored them. And several of them are also sharing classrooms. Every room in the building is rented out to some performer or vendor."

"That makes sense." Charlie agreed. "What are you going to do with the leftover books? Donate them to the library or something?"

"Has Jane not talked to you at all about this? We considered donation, but Jane talked us into another auction. She's auctioning off the bookcases with their contents, and the top 250 bookcases' worth of bids will win. Then, the booksellers who donated books will either negotiate their books back or buy them from the auction winners. Jane's got it all sorted."

Charlie and Seth were both speechless. Seth knew his mother kept him in line, but hadn't thought his mother was capable of something on this scale. And she didn't even tell him Devil's Due was going to be there. Or maybe she did tell him, but he hadn't been paying attention.

Charlie was thinking in terms of dollars. His mother had been PTA president once upon a time, and they had had school carnivals. They were usually pleased when the carnivals broke even. This was so far beyond – and Jane wasn't even PTA president. She had just asked to have one project she could run with – and look how she ran.

They had made their way around the main hallways by this point, and had returned to the glass walls that comprised the bulk of the library. Charlie saw Jane at a desk, mounds of papers and sticky notes on white boards, a messy bun on top of her head, deep in concentration. Just as Seth had raced up to knock on the glass, Jane looked up and waved. Seth opened up the small book return door. "Hi Mom!"

"Hi Seth," he heard her faint reply. "What do you think?"

Seth gave his mom a thumb's up. "Really cool."

"High praise from my young freshman." Jane said. "I'll take it."

You read this one to me and I'll tell Seth he has to shovel the snow path (while we "keep warm" inside).

Ultra-Thin For Her Pleasure

Charlie heard thinly veiled cursing coming from the bathroom the week after the fundraiser. He checked the alarm clock--it was 3 AM. Either Jane was sick, or she was starting. Another hanky-panky-less week for Charlie. He frowned.

"Charlie?" Jane stage-whispered. "Charlie, are you awake?"

Charlie thought about trying to fake sleep, to pretend for just a while longer that everything was right in the dream world of Charlie. But he knew she'd just keep stage whispering louder and louder until he couldn't sleep through it anyway, and by then she'd be furious.

"I'm up. What do you need?" he asked helpfully.

"Charlie, when you went to the store last week, did you get my pads? I don't find any under here."

Charlie could hear Jane rummaging around in the bathroom cabinet.

"Yeah, honey. They were out of your brand, so I got something different. They're in the shopping bag under the sink."

"They were out? Really? Did you ask someone?"

133

Phyl Campbell

"No, I'm not going to ask someone about your stuff."
Never in a million years, Charlie thought to himself.

Charlie heard a plastic bag rustling. Then he heard the
bathroom cabinet door slam. More than once. He was
aware that somehow he'd gotten the 3AM trivia portion of
their evening wrong, but he was the kind of guy who got
feminine products for his wife. It wasn't his fault she
needed them.

He heard the toilet paper roll spin and spin, which was
odd because Jane usually used wet wipes, especially during
her period.

"If I want something done right, I guess I have to do it
myself," Jane was muttering (none too quietly) to herself.
Charlie heard underwear being pulled up and the toilet
flush. He couldn't imagine what she meant. How was it his
fault that the store was out of her favorite brand of
feminine pads? That was not his fault. She could not find
fault with him over that. Except that he knew Jane usually
could. He just didn't know how.

Jane stormed out of the bathroom wearing her t-shirt
and a pair of panties that looked oddly stuffed.

"Is that the pad I bought?" Charlie was shocked. It
said "ultra-thin for her pleasure" on the box. What Jane
had on certainly wasn't ultra-thin, and it didn't look like she
was experiencing pleasure, either.

134

#25 Reasons

"No." Jane drew out the word like it had three syllables. All of them hated men in general and Charlie specifically. "This is a pad made out of toilet paper." Each word was a knife, stabbing Charlie in all his favorite places.

"What's wrong with the ones I bought you?" Charlie knew he shouldn't ask, but the train wreck was leaving the station, and he still hadn't figured out a safe way to jump clear of the tracks.

Jane waddled over past the bed and to the closet. The harsh closet light hurt his eyes when she flicked it on. When she wasn't mad, she tried to shut the door behind her to reduce the light while he was sleeping. She made no such effort now.

"You looked all over for my brand, right?" Jane said in a way that sounded more like an accusation than anything else.

"I said I did." Charlie fumbled. "I mean, I did!"

"And when you didn't find my brand, you looked for the pad that was the most like my brand, right?"

"Of course I did. I did my best. The packages are confusing." Charlie had no idea what Jane's pads looked like. She wrote down her brand and size and that's what he got. Did they actually have pictures on the packaging? Charlie couldn't remember. "Jane, what's wrong with what I got you?"

Phyl Campbell

Jane didn't answer. Charlie could hear her struggling with a pair of sweatpants, which he also couldn't quite figure out. It was too damn early for these guessing games.

Jane emerged from the closet in sweatpants, a different t-shirt, and a half zipped hoodie. She had a pair of socks in her hand.

"Come back to bed. What are you getting dressed for? Are they that bad? Where are you going this time of night?" Again, Charlie knew he was asking the wrong questions. Again, he couldn't stop himself from asking them.

"I have to go to the store, OK Charlie? Since someone didn't tell me the store was out when he went, or put pads back on the list so he didn't have to say the word 'pad' to his *wife of fifteen years*." Jane was so mad she was spitting the words out. "But surely if they were *out* then, they will have had a chance to restock, and won't be *out* now."

Charlie quickly got out of bed. "I'll go, Jane. You're right. They'll have restocked." He still didn't know why the brand was so important, but he was not one to miss a moment of gallantry.

"No, thank you." Jane spit back at him. She walked back to the bathroom, got the bag, and tossed it to Charlie. "Ow!"

#25 Reasons

"You bought me *condoms*, Charlie. You bought me two boxes of fucking *condoms*. I love the irony." Jane's voice dripped with sarcasm and distain. "If I sent you back out now, I'd probably get pregnancy tests. I'd rather go myself."

Charlie's jaw dropped open. How could this have happened? Why couldn't they put pictures on the box or something? Or did they and he just hadn't noticed? He had spent many long, well, minutes trying unsuccessfully to find the purple box with the green wrappers for size 14 and up. He'd bought these because they were extra-large. He remembered that. Why didn't he realize they weren't pads? Why were there so many choices?

So absorbed in his shock and guilt, he didn't even notice when Jane left the room. He just stared. Surely he had not bought his menstruating wife condoms. And when did menopause kick in?

He looked inside the bag. Tiny words like "contraception" and "ribbed" stared back at him, accusingly. Why hadn't he noticed them before? "For her pleasure" mocked him like bad slogans so often do. Definitely false advertising. He should complain to the condom company. As a matter of fact, why couldn't companies package condoms and pads together -- like the pill prescription with the week of placebos?

Phyl Campbell

Charlie sat back down on the bed, hard. He held the evidence of his guilt in his hands.

Why was it so difficult to get women what they wanted? He hadn't worn condoms since his vasectomy. That was years ago. No wonder he got the packages confused. How was he going to return these to the store? No way. He'd look like a total loser. Who buys two boxes of condoms at a time? Who returns them?

It was too damn early. As the garage door lifted, and he heard Jane's car pull out and onto the road, Charlie laid back down and tried to think of something pleasant. It took him a while to get back to sleep.

Maybe I should read this part to you. When you find this one – let me know and maybe I will.

Double Painful Double Date

Jane studied her reflection in the mirror. "Charlie? Do you think --"

"No way." Charlie cut her off. "I am not answering questions about your appearance. You are sexy and gorgeous and wonderful and we are going to be late." Jane appeared to have forgiven him for last week's mishap, but it was Valentine's Day and he wasn't taking any chances – which included sticking his neck out any further than he had to.

"I was going to ask you if you thought you could bring my black pumps out of the closet. You know, since you're standing right there and I'm still trying to figure out what to do with this mop on my head."

"Oh. Well, that's different." Charlie couldn't tell whether she was being truthful or not, but he supposed she could. Charlie disappeared further into the walk-in closet. "Pumps. Pumps. Which ones do you want? The sandal looking things? Or the boots?"

"No, the – oh, never mind. I'll get them." Jane sighed. She had more pairs of shoes than Charlie did, but few compared to most women. Didn't most guys know the difference between pumps, sandals, and boots? Jane went to the closet and retrieved the shoes. "I should be helping Amy get ready."

"Did she ask you to?"

"Well, no. But it's just what you do."

"I have helped no man prepare for a date."

"She's like my sister. It's what you do for family, maybe."

"I'm still debating whether or not I'll help Seth when the time comes."

"Maybe it's a woman thing you wouldn't understand."

Charlie put his finger on his nose. "Ding! Ding! Give the lady a prize!" He grinned cheezily at her, wondering if he was pushing his luck too far. "But seriously, it's just dinner."

"It's our first time to meet this guy. If things go well with us, she may be introducing him to her parents."

"It's that serious already?"

"Apparently. She really likes him."

"What does he do again?"

"She didn't say." Jane stopped for a moment, shoe in hand. "It's funny. She's been really vague about him this whole time. It's not like her."

"No pictures, no nothing?"

#25 Reasons

"Now that you mention it, no. She's got selfies, of course, at bars and clubs with people around. It never occurred to me that I hadn't seen him. She hasn't stopped talking about him."

"Well, how long has it been?"

"A few months, I think. Is that right? It was before Christmas, but after my birthday."

All of a sudden, Charlie had a really bad feeling.

"What did you say his name was again?"

"She just calls him by pet names. That's really weird. Huh. I hadn't given it much thought. Maybe he's really short."

Maybe he's a real piece of work. Charlie thought.

"So why us?" He asked. "It's only been a few months, like you said. And we're not old enough to stand in for Amy's parents. Doesn't Amy have other single friends to double date with?"

"We have a solid relationship. Amy said she had a rocky start with this one, and given the last guy I set her up with, that's saying something. She says when she doubles with other singles, everyone is so self-involved that it doesn't go well and she can't figure out why. Said they're fine when they're alone, but that doesn't make for a good partnership." Jane finished putting in her earring and went

143

to Charlie. She put her hand on his shoulder and looked up at him. "She wants what we have, Charlie."

Charlie looked down at Jane and smiled. "Amy knows I'm an awful judge of character, right? That I have two left feet? That even my taste in music is questionable?"

"Charlie. You're not trying to get out of this, are you?"

"Of course I am. Dressing up. Nice restaurant. Lack of mechanically minded television programming." *Not to mention a suspicion. Make that a really bad feeling.*

"Is that all it is?" Jane put both hands on his shoulders and turned her head slightly with a quizzical look.

Charlie put his hands over his wife's. "You know me, honey. Fancy places. Fine dining where I need to know the proper place for my napkin, lots of people around? And Seth! What about Seth? It's not good for us to leave him all alone. Maybe I should just stay home."

"Seth is fourteen years old and totally capable of fending for himself for an evening. It will be good for us to go out for a night on the town. Besides, it's Valentine's Day."

"Another fake commercial holiday for the greeting card companies."

"You're taking me to dinner."

"Well, then, let's go. Just the two of us."

#25 Reasons

"Charlie. For Pete's sake. You're being positively weird."

Charlie hoped he was wrong. But all he could think was this was bad. This was very, very bad.

Charlie's fear was confirmed when they met Peter – in a suit, no less, outside the restaurant on the crowded city square. Jane would never believe he hadn't known, and if Peter hurt Amy, she would never forgive him. Charlie busied himself taking in the architecture – strong red brick buildings with heavy wooden doors and two and three step stoops that were in no way ADA compliant. The square was situated on the edge of the college campus property, and the storefronts were a mix of student funk and alumni sophistication.

"Peter, is that you? You're looking dapper this evening. Planning to break some poor call girl's heart tonight?"

"Jane, you look lovely." Peter uncharacteristically replied. "I'm glad Charlie's taking such good care of you."

"I take care of myself, and Charlie takes care of Charlie." Jane retorted. She was somewhat taken aback by the polite gesture but recovered quickly. "But thank you. Seriously, though. What are you doing here, and tonight of all nights?"

"My date is introducing me to some friends tonight. She's inside. I had to park the car."

Charlie's head jerked. "You drove her yourself?"

Charlie could tell Jane was itching to say something else, but not if he could help it. He still hoped by some miracle he was wrong and Peter's presence was just a coincidence. But he was genuinely surprised Peter wasn't making Amy hoof the same distance from the parking garage.

"Of course, Charlie. I'm not a complete moron. Too many things can happen to a shiny Beemer sitting on a busy street like this, so I dropped her off first and I just walked back." Then Peter realized that they were standing in front of Jane's car. "But I'm sure you've got a sturdy ride there. You shouldn't have any problems."

Jane showed moderate signs of choking, but whether it was from the thinly veiled insult or the back-handed compliment, Charlie couldn't be sure. Charlie also wasn't sure how Peter meant it, which was unusual.

"Anyway, I've got to be going. I don't want to keep Amy waiting."

"Amy?" Jane asked, with a slight hint of anger.

"Yeah. Amy Baxter. She's on the police force. Maybe you know her?"

#25 Reasons

Before Jane could fire back a reply, Charlie said. "Peter. You don't want to keep your lady friend waiting. Jane, can you come here for a minute, please?"

"See you later, Charlie." Peter said, oblivious to the storm rising in Jane's eyes. "Nice to see you again, Jane." He turned and walked briskly up to the stoop, opened the heavy wooden door, and let himself inside.

Charlie met Jane halfway around the car.

"How could you not tell me?!"

"I swear. I didn't even suspect until you didn't know where he worked. Some guys at work have been harassing Peter about canceling poker night, but I didn't"

"How else do you make that leap, Charlie? What am I going to tell Amy? She's going to be heartbroken."

"The better question is, Jane, why didn't Amy tell you? Think about it. Amy tells you everything. Yet after more than a month of dating, you've never seen a picture of this guy. You didn't know his name or where he worked. Amy knew how you – how we – felt about Peter. But she's with him and we have to be supportive until he screws up or they're married like us. I was a moron once, too, you know. Before you fixed me." He smiled hopefully at her.

"You're still a moron."

"Always and forever, my love."

147

Jane didn't want to say that Charlie very likely had a point, but he did. She just thought she hadn't been paying attention to Amy, and she'd felt bad about that. Amy got excited about a lot of guys that crashed and burned. After a while, they all sort of ran together.

"But – Peter? 'Here's a sex toy, I'm sure you won't need directions' – Peter?"

"That didn't turn out all bad."

"We had to cut you out of it!"

"True. Thanks again for the caution you exercised with the scissors, by the way."

"I"

"I know, honey. But I've also never seen Peter give you a compliment before. I've never seen him put a lady before his car. Maybe Amy is just right for him. Goodness knows you were right for me."

"I don't like it."

"I don't like it, either, Jane. But let's give them a shot and a chance to explain themselves before we kick them to the curb. OK?"

"And you honestly didn't know."

"Baby, until we walk though those doors and see Amy – our Amy – holding hands or whatever with Peter," Charlie shook his head in bewilderment. "Peter. Until we do that, I still don't know, won't know, and can hope against hope that we're wrong. Maybe there's another Amy in booking or something and then we'll both have jumped to the wrong conclusion. Maybe it's all a big coincidence, and Amy is here with someone else."

The front door of the restaurant opened. Amy stood on the stoop and pressed her hands on the railing, leaning out. "Hey, are you guys coming? I'm starving!"

"Be right there!" Charlie called over what he expected would have been other words from Jane. He turned Jane around to face Amy, wrapped her in a hug, and whispered into her ear. "Look how happy she is, Jane. Support your friend."

"Be right there!" Jane called. She turned back around. "Charlie. Are you sure about this?"

"Not one bit. But c'mon. Cat's most likely out of the bag, and I'm hungry, too."

Amy looked like a mermaid out of water in her figure flattering blue dress and matching heels. Her blonde hair, normally pulled back into a bun or ponytail for work, was now loose and hung in soft waves about her shoulders. And while Amy was not a girl to go without makeup, tonight it was obvious she'd put extra effort into its application. Put simply, she glowed. But Jane could see her nerves as she and Charlie walked over to the standing table.

149

"I ordered drinks from the counter while we wait for a table. Sodas for the both of you. My guy's waiting on them. They're super busy tonight. Unless Charlie – do you want something stronger?"

"Nah, I'm good with soda." Charlie said. "But if you want me to go away so you can talk to Jane, I can do that."

"Please?"

"Gone." Charlie kissed the side of Jane's head and went to find Peter's hiding spot.

"So..." Amy said.

"So why didn't you just tell me it was Peter?"

"Wait – how did you find out?"

"We met him outside after he parked the car. But, really, Amy – why keep me in the dark?"

"I knew what you'd think – what you'd say. When we first went out, I didn't expect there to be a second date. I mean, how can you be attracted to someone who loves your handcuffs more than your smile? But we started hanging out more, and then dating more seriously, and then I just didn't know how to tell you without"

"Without letting me know you'd basically lied to me?"

"I *evaded* the truth." Amy admitted. "And only because I didn't want you to be hurt if I made my own judgment about him – or feel guilty if it didn't work out."

"Why would I feel guilty?"

#25 Reasons

"Well, do you remember your unbirthday?"

"I try not to."

"Well, that was our first conversation. Mine and Peter's. He thought I was you, and wouldn't give up any information on Charlie. He didn't want to be the one to spoil the surprise."

"You never told me that!"

"At the time, it didn't mean anything. But then I guess Charlie told the guys at work about what happened, and Peter brought me flowers for scaring Charlie by pointing a gun at him. I think he meant it as a joke. He didn't expect me to be pretty, he said." Amy giggled with embarrassment at the memory.

"Awww – that's sweet!" Jane admitted. "Still, pick-up lines have never been Peter's problem, from what I've heard. So then what happened?"

"We went on a date." Peter said, handing a glass of something bubbly to Amy. Charlie was there, too, with something dark and fizzy for Jane. "And one of my exes was there serving. She was not happy to see me."

"You can say that again." Amy said with a chuckle.

"She was not happy to see me." Peter said again, and they both laughed.

Charlie looked over at Jane and subtly raised an eyebrow. This was Peter – the womanizing coworker who gave horrid romantic advice? It didn't seem like the same guy. The feeling was akin to telling someone they were getting a Rottweiler and then handing them a tiny puppy. Still plausible, not false – if the puppy was a Rottweiler -- but unexpected.

Jane cleared her throat. "So, how can I put this delicately, you know about Peter's, uhm"

"Sexual proclivity? Womanizing? Man-whoring?" Amy laughed. "Yeah. Pretty hard for him to hide his past from me. There's been an ex in nearly every restaurant he's taken me to."

"But that's what it is," Peter protested. "Past."

"Is it the cop thing?" Charlie wanted to know.

"Yeah, partly." Peter grinned and elbowed Charlie playfully. "It's great to have a woman who comes with her own cuffs and uniform."

"And I like Peter's experience." Amy said matter-of-factly. "I like a guy confident enough in his skills that he isn't questioning his performance all the time. Apparently, I have a LOT of exes to thank for that."

"And it doesn't bother you?" Jane asked. "No offense, Peter."

"None taken."

#25 Reasons

"All that was before me. It's not like we were in a relationship and he was cheating on me. I DID make him get checked out and tested for everything."

"And she does mean everything." Peter groaned in an aside to Charlie, who chuckled.

"So the cheetah can change his spots?" Jane said, eyes on Peter though the question was directed at Amy.

"I keep my spots, but I relocated from the zoo."

"He's not an animal, Jane."

"It's alright, Amy. Jane probably owes me three or four really good digs at least. Charlie knows why if she doesn't."

"Charlie?" Amy asked.

"Man, is our table ready yet? Did you tell them you were starving, Amy?" Charlie asked, avoiding her question and changing the subject completely.

"Tell me about it," Peter said, playing along. "Do you two come here often?"

The waiter came to seat them then and they enjoyed dinner, chatting like old friends – though Charlie noticed Jane was a little more reserved and a little more on edge than usual. If the others noticed, they made no comment.

Phyl Campbell

And then dinner was over and Charlie drove Jane home.

"I am so glad we don't have to do that anymore." Jane finally said when Charlie was parking the car in the driveway at home.

"Do what?"

"Dating."

Charlie snorted.

"Do you remember our first date? It was Valentine's Day then, too. You weren't going to get a second."

"But I did."

Jane laughed. "Yeah. You wore me down."

"I took you to that great seafood restaurant."

"Before you found out I was allergic to shellfish."

"Well, yeah. But I saved you just in time."

"I was starving."

"And we hit that drive-thru."

"Hooray," Jane dead-panned. "Valentine's Day at the drive-thru."

"And then I took you to the bookstore."

"Yeah. You did."

"Is that what this is about? The books?"

"Shut up, Charlie." Jane said. "Not everything is about the books."

154

"But you just said."

"Charlie, you were right when you told me to listen to Amy."

"I was what?"

"You were right. I can say it. I don't choke on the words."

"I didn't say you did."

"As though I don't know your smirks." Jane noticed Charlie's face get red, amazed she could still figure him out and hoping she could use that shocked silence to get him to really hear her. "But what I was getting at is that you told me to listen to Amy. I did, and you were right. And now I want you to listen to me."

"I do listen to you, Jane."

"The bookstore meant a lot to me because we shared a love of books. We used to do a lot of things together. And now we don't. We do things as a threesome or you and Seth or me and Seth. Or we are all busy going our separate ways."

"Is that why you were so quiet tonight? I thought you were mad at Peter."

"No. If Amy doesn't blame me for setting the two of them up, when I obviously had nothing to do with it, then I'm fine. She's a grown woman. No. I was thinking about us."

"I thought you were happy not to be dating anymore."

"I'm happy not to be trying to find someone at our age. We weren't exactly spring chickens when we met, Charlie, but we were still young enough that inexperience was more expected. Did you hear Amy talking about Peter being a pro? Compare that to our first time."

"Do I have to?" Charlie groaned.

"No." Jane laughed. "Our first time was sweet."

"It's nothing at all like they do it in your books."

"You're right. Some things don't belong in books."

"Like the time we tried it in the back of the pick up?"

"Oh, crap. My butt still hurts!" Jane laughed.

"Sorry."

They both laughed at private memories of their time together.

The next thing they knew, the windows were foggy. Laughter wasn't the only reason they were both out of breath.

"I think we should go inside, Mrs. Hart."

"Absolutely, Mr. Hart."

Read me a page 69 that I've marked and maybe you'll get a 69.

Doggie Style

"Time for you to be na-ked," Charlie sing-songed. He was holding a paperback book in one hand, the front cover pressed against the back in a way that was terrible for its spine. "I found page sixty-ni-ine." His glee was, well, odd for a man of his age, education, and size.

Jane looked up from her side of the bed, annoyed that her novel had been interrupted. "What page sixty-nine? I didn't mark a page sixty-nine." And she'd checked – three times – just to make sure.

"You didn't have to. It's your book. I found it myself. All your books have a page sixty-nine. Isn't it wonderful?" Charlie set the book on his side of the bed, out of Jane's reach. He waved the offending sticky note in front of her nose. Then he alternated between a bizarre form of striptease and rolling down his blankets to the foot of the bed.

"Give me that." Jane lunged over and grabbed the sticky note mid strip-and-roll. "It says that I marked. It's very clear."

"Oh, there's a mark on the book." Half-naked Charlie gleefully showed Jane where she'd written her name – marking the book. "Do you deny this mark?"

"Give me that, too." Jane snatched the book from Charlie, a blush creeping up her cheeks. Charlie was too entangled to stop her. "Charlie. This isn't a romance. This is science fiction. The female character in this one is a robot. A. Robot." Jane emphasized.

"A very limber robot." Charlie agreed.

"And I am NOT a very limber wife. Nor am I impressed. Misogynistic robot loving men? Real women barely even show up in this one."

"It's your book." Charlie rebutted with a grin. "You said if I read your books -- you said if I worked a little harder to make it good for you -- we'd have more sex. So I, like a good doggie, am reading your books. I really like this one."

"This is not what I meant by romance."

"But it is romantic. And you marked it. And it's page sixty-nine. Pay up."

"Ugh. There's so much sex in this one. I ought to have gotten rid of it. You should – especially before Seth finds it. That's a conversation I don't want to be having later."

"Oh, I'll keep Seth from finding it." Charlie said, swiping the book back from Jane. "It's staying right here by me."

Jane wasn't sure about that. She also wasn't sure that she could handle a playful, giddy husband. Making her laugh was one thing. This was, in a word, unsettling. She tried to find the place in the novel where she'd left off.

Charlie was not about to be ignored.

"Come on, Jane." He cajoled. "Be a sport."

"We both hate sports."

"I don't hate hockey."

"I hate all sports enough for both of us."

Charlie crawled across the bed on his hands and knees. If a man could crawl and frolic at the same time, well, that's what Charlie was doing. Then he got down on his elbows and licked the side of Jane's face from the bottom of her chin to the top of her head.

"Ewwwwww! What the hell, Charlie?"

"C'mon, Jane. Charlie wants you to play with his bone." He wiggled his tailbone in the air for effect.

Jane burst out laughing. "And I assume puppy dog eyes are next?"

Charlie obliged. "Pet me, Jane. Pet me. I'll be your best friend."

"Dogs are man's best friend. Not a lady's."

161

"Lady my ass, Jane. C'mon. Play with my bone. Please, Jane? We don't even have to do it like the book."

"Two nights of dishes."

Charlie cocked his head to the side, doggie-style. "What?"

"Two nights of dishes."

"But I cook." Charlie protested. "And this is about the books. It's not fair for you to add other conditions."

"You leave a huge mess when you cook. And this is using the books for you, not for me. You deliberately found a loophole in my plan."

"You deliberately made a sticky note about sixty-nines and then didn't mark any page sixty-nine."

"You noticed that, huh?"

"You admitted it."

Jane sighed. It had been funny at the time, but now it looked like she would have to put her mouth where...

"I'd make it good for you, Jane."

Jane ignored this.

"I promise. I don't ask for much, Jane."

Jane felt this was debatable, but Charlie looked so pitiful she knew she would give in. But not yet. "So if you want to get freaky tonight, you get dish duty for the next two nights. And no pawning it off on Seth, either."

"Ruh roh." Charlie waggled his butt happily anyway.

#25 Reasons

"I mean it. He's got enough stuff with school, homework, and band practice."

"But, but," Charlie whined in a very unmanly fashion. "But Charlie's been a good doggie. He needs some lovin', Jane. Some doggone lovin'." His hind end resumed its wagging.

"Suit yourself." Trying to stifle her laughter, Jane rolled over and pretended to sleep. Charlie resumed licking her face.

"Ewww! Ewww! Ewww! Eww! Eww!" Jane squealed.

"You know you wanna play with my bone, Jane."

"Dishes!"

Charlie resumed licking her face.

"All right! All right! All right! Would you stop that?"

"All right!" Charlie cheered.

"You're going to wake up Seth."

"Nope. Charlie's a good doggie. A quiet doggie." His rump started to wag again.

"Since when did you think I was into bestiality?"

"Jane likes it doggie style."

"I thought you wanted a sixty-nine?"

"Charlie doesn't give a damn. Charlie just wants lovin'."

"Does Charlie always talk about himself in the third person?" Jane teased.

Phyl Campbell

Charlie let his tongue roll out of his mouth and panted in response.

"And Seth wonders why we're never getting a dog." Jane grumbled, but not in an angry way. Doggie style was much easier to swallow than a sixty-nine, anyway.

Charlie rolled over and played dead. Then Jane got in some licks of her own.

The reader of this passage is entitled to one long winter's nap with the woman he loves. Unless the woman is NOT me, in which case...

Pop Up Porn

Charlie worked very hard at his job. Even so, he often brought work home with him. He tried to be courteous and work in the upstairs bedroom so that Jane and Seth could watch prime-time TV downstairs undisturbed – and without disturbing him. He also watched movies or shows on his laptop. It had gotten to be quite a habit.

Jane wanted him to come out to watch the shows, but he spent the whole time asking questions because he'd missed previous episodes. Then Jane or Seth would "shush" him, he'd be confused and mad, and would retreat to the bedroom. He really hadn't been that interested in the first place.

However, Jane also tried to "visit" Charlie during her commercials, which normally meant that Charlie had to keep his business window available at a moment's notice and his entertainment window minimized in the same moment.

On Tuesday, however, Jane happened to find a rather racy parade of scantily clad women on Charlie's computer while he was in the shower.

Honestly, Jane had no Charlie was taking so many women to his bed. Was this what he was working so hard on? Was he having to shower off his hard on? Jane laughed, then groaned at her play on words. It didn't solve her problem. Did she have a problem? She wasn't sure.

Charlie took short showers, so there was no·need to turn off the laptop if he was coming back to it. On the other hand, why leave this on for Jane to find? Was he hinting to her? Was this payback for the books? And how did Jane feel about it?

On the one hand, what audacity Charlie had not to just come out and say what he wanted! On the other hand, perhaps he never meant for Jane to see what digital images and videos existed on his computer. Perhaps he thought he'd be quicker, or that she was too involved downstairs to come up?

Maybe Charlie knew that any request for Jane to be similarly attired and dancing around foolishly would be met with Jane's wifely Evil Eye, and these harmless women scampering across the screen were just harmless images on a man's computer. Many men in healthy monogamous relationships viewed porn from time to time. Charlie was a healthy virile male, entitled to the occasional screen of titillation. And this wasn't even porn – yet.

#25 Reasons

Sadly, anyone thinking that Jane would accept any logical explanation about scantily clad women on Charlie's computer simply does not understand Jane Hart.

She heard the water turn off, and had only seconds to plan her course of action. She quickly ducked into the closet, tossed off her clothes, threw on – well, she tried to throw on – a snug piece of lingerie that she'd outgrown two depressing sizes ago, and jumped back onto the bed just as Charlie opened the door from the bathroom to their bedroom.

"Well, hello there, sexy." Charlie grinned.

Jane noticed how he had one towel wrapped at his waist and another hung from his shoulders. When his hair was wet, like it was now, his balding pate was most obvious. Jane tried not to be caught staring. She knew he couldn't help it any more than either of them were helping keep their love handles on the slim and trim side. She had to stay focused.

"Who, me?" Jane breathed, then school-girl giggled in a way she knew aroused her husband and lover.

"No one else in the bed now, is there?" Charlie teased.

So he knew. He had set her up. Angry tears threatened the corners of Jane's eyes.

"Wanna bet?" Jane slung her husband's laptop around to reveal her scantily clad prancing bed mates. "I know they

Phyl Campbell

look better than I do, especially given the child I bore you. But the LEAST you could do Charlie is keep your FILTH out of OUR BED!" Jane jumped up, ran to the bathroom her husband had just exited, and slammed the door.

It was just a joke, wasn't it? She wasn't really that mad – was she? Hot tears streamed down her face. There was a logical explanation. Their love wasn't really over. Internet porn was so much better than finding a real younger woman in her bed. But Jane didn't like the idea of being replaced by megabytes or pixels. Was the internet porn a joke – or was she?

"Jane? Jane?" Charlie knocked on the other side of the door.

Jane couldn't speak. He felt bad to be caught. Well, he should, she thought. He should feel bad. All the same, it was no wonder to Jane that laptops and smart phones rarely existed in the romances she read. Men didn't bring home dirty magazines in those books, either – though sometimes parents found them in bedrooms of their teenage boys.

Jane wasn't one of those shrinking violets who trapped men into a bad marriage. If he wanted something more, she'd try to find a way to be OK with it. Obviously, the books alone weren't working. What else could she do?

170

#25 Reasons

And now here she was, crying on the toilet seat of her bathroom, dressed in too small lingerie, trapped. She couldn't get to her clothes without walking past Charlie. Seth would have to finish *Siblingitis* without her. It was a shame. She really wanted to know if Tabitha and Sharon would be able to work out their differences after they'd both slept with the sleazy doctor.

But she knew she couldn't leave the bathroom until Charlie was snoring. She'd dug her heels in, and now it was too late.

Alone in the bedroom, Charlie took exactly three minutes to assess the damage he'd done. He hated it when pop up ads kept his movie from loading. The girls weren't even all that cute. They looked half-starved. No sense telling Jane that when she was upset, though. And no sense trying to talk to Jane when she was this upset. Forget finishing his movie, either, that would just make her madder. So while Jane tried to silence her sobs over the toilet bowl, Charlie shut off his movie, shut down his laptop, and went to sleep.

We can try this
when Seth is
spending the night
at a friend's house.

Twenty Questions with a Teenager

"Mom, what are all these books for?" Seth asked. He was out of school for Spring Break, but Charlie still had to work, so Jane intended to make him useful.

"They're for your father."

"They don't look like his."

"Don't worry about it."

"But you always tell me to keep my stuff in my room."

"This is his room. They're all his rooms. And my rooms. Unless you've got a rent check for me?"

"Nah, I'm good. So why…"

"Is your homework done?"

"Don't have any. It's Spring Break."

"No term papers coming up? No projects? Are you supposed to do an experiment for Science Fair?"

"I don't think so."

Jane sighed. Sunday night was going to be revealing, she was sure, but the school didn't send home notices like they did when Seth was little. He was expected to keep up with it. Clearly the Powers That Be did not have children of their own.

"What book are you reading?"

"I left it at school."

"Is it a popular book? Can we check out another copy from the library for you?"

"Sure. Maybe."

"What's it called?"

"I don't know."

"How can I replace the book you left at school if you can't tell me what it was?"

"It's OK." Seth picked up a book that Jane never wanted to look at in the light of day. "This one looks interesting. I like robots."

"No!" Jane jumped up and snatched the book out of Seth's surprised hands.

"What's the big deal, mom? It's a robot book."

Jane was thoroughly busted. Mothers should never freak out in front of their kids. She sat, speechless, the book in her lap. And in that minute she took to speak, she thought of at least five ways to murder Charlie, who'd *promised* to keep the book from Seth. Piecrust promise. She learned that phrase when she'd played Mary Poppins in musical theatre class in college.

"Mom? Mom, are you OK?"

"Mm-hmm." She could really use a spoonful of sugar right now. Or for Charlie to come home early and clean up his mess.

#25 Reasons

"You don't look OK." Seth insisted.

Jane looked up at Seth, but still didn't trust herself to open her mouth.

"Mom. Why can't I read that robot book?"

Jane took a deep breath. *Mary Poppins. Mary Poppins. Mary Poppins.* Then she sucked in another breath and said, "I'm sorry Seth. I shouldn't have over-reacted like that. But this is not a book about robots." And she decided to go for broke. "This is a book about a man that has sex with a robot."

"Gross! Mom! Why does Dad have a book like that?"

"Actually, it's mine."

Seth's eyes bugged out. "But you're my mom. Moms don't like that kind of stuff."

Jane let out a short laugh. "Sometimes we do."

"And you want Dad to read that?"

An axe would be too messy. Guns would appear pre-meditated. No jury in the world would convict me. 'I'm sorry, your Honor, but he swore Seth was never going to find that book and that I didn't have to worry. I really was thinking about the well-being of my impressionable son.' Maybe cut the line on his brakes?

"It seemed like a good idea at the time."

"Why?"

"Boy, you're full of questions today!"

"That's not an answer."

175

Jane hated it when Seth used her words against her. "Ok. I'm going to level with you. You're old enough to get a straight answer. Dad and I have been married a long time. Sometimes people who've been married a long time get in a rut."

"A rut? What's that?"

"A rut's a worn spot in the road left by the weight of vehicles – bikes and cars and trucks and stuff."

"So you're doing it in the car? That's disgusting!"

"No, no – sorry. I'm not explaining this very well. A rut is when the same thing happens over and over. It's boring. But the thing about ruts it that you can get stuck in them. Or feel stuck in them. Stuck in the boring and stuck in the same-ness. You have a rut when you go to school every day and tell me you aren't learning anything. I think you're in a video game rut and should spend more time outside. You follow that?"

"I guess so. So are you going to divorce Dad?"

"He's not that lucky. I've got my ball and chain on him and it's staying."

Jane's cheeky response was met with Seth's wide grin. He relaxed almost instantly.

"So you have a book about robots having sex?"

"Well, about a man having sex with a robot."

"That is so gross. So why can't I read it?"

#25 Reasons

Jane exhaled disgustedly. "I think you're too young to be reading books about sex. And given how adult males react to your dad having these books around, I don't even want to think about what other kids at school might say."

"So? Who cares about them? Anyway, I could read it here at home."

"Seth? Do you really want to read a book about a robot having sex?"

"I don't know. It could be interesting. You like it."

"I'm older and I'm married. I like a lot of stuff you don't."

"I see sex in movies and stuff sometimes. It's not that big a deal, Mom. It's just sex."

Jane's shoulders slumped and she sighed again. "Yeah. There's a lot of sex and violence on TV and movies. And your dad and I don't censor a lot of it. We watch together. We talk about what's going on. You know you can always come to us with questions and we aren't going to judge or make fun of you for having them. And we'll always answer the best we can."

"I know all that."

"Maybe your dad and I think there's so much sex on the TV that you're kind of immune to it. And thanks to the FCC, actors have to leave a lot up to the viewers' imaginations. You can close your eyes and open them again after the commercial break, or when you hear a different conversation. It's harder to overlook sex in books. At least, it is until you get the hang of it. And sex in books is harder to forget about."

"Why?"

Jane sucked in a lot of air before she answered.

"That's another great question. I don't have an answer for that. Maybe it's just my opinion. Maybe it's the fact that you can't close your eyes or skip forward out of a sex scene without – usually – missing something important."

"Like what?"

"Depends on the book."

"Oh.

"Maybe I should have sat down with you and had this talk in August."

"We already had the talk about boy parts and girl parts and sex, Mom."

"I know, but about this. About the books. The first day you found out about the books."

"Dad thinks they're stupid."

"I know."

"So why do you like them?"

Jane nodded. "Honestly – I'm still trying to figure that out myself. I like the settings. I like being able to relate to everyday people in them – and the occasional robot, of course. And romance novels almost always have happy endings. I could use some of that simplicity – that no matter how out of control everything gets, it's all going to get resolved. That's a good mantra for life, you know."

"But I've seen you reading them. Sometimes you still cry. Why would you cry if the ending was happy?"

"For the same reason that people cry at weddings and laugh at funerals."

"And why is that?"

"Honestly? I don't know. Emotional release, maybe?"

"Maybe. And it's ok to say you don't know, Mom. I can handle it when you're honest with me. I also kinda like that you don't know everything. It means I don't have to know everything. Even though I do, of course."

"Seth?"

"Yeah, Mom?"

"I'm glad we talked. I hope you know you can always ask me anything."

"Yeah, Mom. Sure."

"Seth?"

"Yeah?"

"Because your dad and I know you're not a little kid anymore, I'm not going to tell you not to read the robot book if you really want to. I don't think it will make sense to you on an emotional level, but you're right that you

179

watch movies and TV shows with sex. And if your dad and I censored what you read, I think you'd just try to get sneakier about reading it behind our backs. I don't want that."

"Ok. Hey – can I go to Erik's house for lunch today?"

"Were you invited or are you asking if you can ask?"

"Yes." Seth's eyes twinkled mischievously.

Jane snorted. "Text Erik and make sure it's ok with his mom. I want to see the text in case he says yes and his mother didn't."

"Ok."

And Seth was gone again. The books remained in their stack on the table beside the couch. Jane walked over to them. The dreaded page sixty-nine was the last passage Charlie had read to her. Or had there been one after that? She was still embarrassed about her reaction to the pop up ad she thought was Charlie watching porn. He never apologized – not that she'd given him a chance to. Had she not gotten the same pop-up ad, she might still be holding a grudge. Fifteen years was a long time to be married – too long for getting mad about stupid, petty things like pop-up ads.

The house had been chilly for March – and it was partially her fault. The books and the sticky notes were a bad idea. She wasn't a robot and neither was Charlie. She

180

#25 Reasons

picked up the stack of books and returned them to their places on the bookshelf. Maybe she would suggest going out to dinner tonight. Something different. Something to signal to Charlie that they were ok.

An Unwelcome Visitor

Charlie hated funerals. He didn't see the point. The dead person was, well, dead – and unlikely to care whether someone showed up to look at her in a casket with embalming fluid. In fact, Charlie figured that dead people would have much better things to do than hang around their own funerals.

Moreover, why do women insist on everybody dressing up for funerals? When women are normally upset, like losing a job or a bad breakup, they put on pairs of sweatpants and dig the ice cream out of the freezer. So when it's really bad – no coming back to the living bad – why do they insist on Sunday best? They're not the ones in the casket. Why must guys don suits, standing around a dead body like a group of Italian gangsters who ordered the hit in the first place? The whole thing was ridiculous – getting all dressed up to put a dead body which had been pumped full of chemicals into fresh dirt. He smirked that there WAS an appropriate suit for that – the one in his car, waiting for him. He hated putting off the insulation project two weekends in a row, but husbands and fathers made compromises for their wives and children. Charlie just hoped he didn't have to make too many more compromises, because that insulation wasn't going to blow itself. No matter who died.

It wasn't that Charlie objected to the deceased – Jane's great aunt Marjorie was a great lady. High spirited. Classy. She was a great conversationalist and a great cook. She loved books, and often passed her favorites down to Jane. Sometimes Charlie really liked that. She'd liked him, too – which was not something he could say about all the members of Jane's family. What was it about in-laws? At least they all could agree to love Seth. That was something.

So Charlie tried not to tug at his tie too much or complain too much about the fact that he was uncomfortable. He knew some men wore three-piece suits to the office every day – bankers, lawyers – schmucks, if you asked Charlie. It was bad enough that he was expected to dress up for expos and conferences.

Beside him, Seth was not trying to hide his discomfort. His index finger hooked once again – none too inconspicuously – to allow him another inch between his neck and his noose. And his phone snuck out of his blazer pocket every time he thought Charlie was blocking his mother's view of him. Charlie was trying his best to be unhelpful in this regard. He loved his son, but had no intention of risking Jane's ire or taking the fall for it. Seth's mother was going to catch him, and when he did, Charlie would happily throw his son under that bus.

Then the music started. Six men rolled great aunt Marjorie down the aisle of the chapel. They lifted the casket to walk the short steps to the front of the chapel altar and placed her casket on the platform.

"Dad?"

"Yes, Seth."

"How do they know it won't collapse?"

"What?"

"The platform. I saw them setting it up earlier. How do they know it won't buckle and fall?"

Charlie remembered wondering the same thing as a younger man. He hadn't ever gotten anyone to explain it fully to him.

"Well..." he started to say, stalling.

"Shhh!" Jane elbowed Charlie. "Show some respect."

"He had a question."

"Shhh!"

Luckily, not everyone took funerals as seriously as Jane did. The cousin on Seth's other side – Jim or Jonathon or whatever his name was – started whispering to Seth about hydraulics, levers, and pivot points. Charlie was a little jealous. Not only could he not hear the full explanation, but Jane would never fuss at someone from her extended family, and now Seth could get away with talking, too.

The service was in full swing when Charlie was roused from his daydreaming by strangled gasps and startled shrieks.

"Was that a cat?"

"I don't think so."

"How the hell did that get in here?"

The best, and yet worst, comment was a little girl near the front who simply chirped "Pepe!"

There was no mistake. A skunk was wandering unsteadily up the aisle. It made its way to the platform where great-aunt Marjorie lay in repose. It wandered around the legs of the hydraulic platform, the stretched out its front feet, cat-like, to lay in a ball under the casket.

"Oh, man! What if it hit a lever and the platform came down and smooshed it?" Seth asked excitedly.

"Seth! That's not funny!" Jane hissed.

Charlie silently high-fived his son. The idea was hilarious.

The officiator stopped. The funeral stopped. Fifty pairs of mourners' eyes fixated just under the casket at the black and white rodent who'd found a quiet place to nap. All the hinges, hydraulics, bolts and nuts did not offer a clear path to removing the rodent from a safe distance. No one wanted to risk their Sunday best getting sprayed. A few people got out their phones and started taking pictures. Jane could not stop Seth from searching "skunk funeral" on his own phone. Of course, when he found video, inspiration struck, and he switched his phone over, cursing himself for not catching the footage of Pepe coming up the aisle.

The funeral director was at a loss for words. They had action plans for fire drills and bad weather, disgruntled relatives and unruly protesters. A sleeping skunk fit none of these protocols. Should they evacuate? Finish the service? Let sleeping skunks lie? They really just didn't know.

But Charlie knew. "Jane, I'll be right back."

"What?"

"Don't let anyone else go near the skunk. I've just got to go get something out of the car."

"OK." Jane had no idea what was in the car besides Seth's swim trunks and beach towel that she'd been nagging him to get out of the car since school started and the pool closed. A few more weeks, and the pool would reopen, so what was the point? There were also about twenty plastic bags she'd been meaning to take to recycle at the grocery store. She hoped Charlie didn't think he was going to catch the skunk and toss it in a plastic bag. Or make a suit of plastic bags? Perhaps better than nothing, but she didn't

187

see it going well. She'd just have to sit and wait like everyone else.

More than one set of in-laws saw Charlie leave. Jane and Seth got some looks that were part sympathy and part critical judgment. Jane glared right back at them. Charlie had his faults, sure, but he wasn't just standing around like a bump on a log. "He's coming back!" she snapped at them. Then she kept her eyes forward, presuming to keep them on the altar, casket, or skunk.

Several minutes later, when Jane had almost started to wonder whether Charlie would return, he did – in a very different kind of suit. With her eyes forward, Jane didn't see him come in.

"What is he wearing?"

"Mommy, look at the spaceman!"

Jane couldn't stop herself from turning around. Yes, Charlie did resemble a spaceman in a hazmat suit. He held Seth's beach towel in his hands.

"A hazmat suit? Charlie – where did you get a hazmat suit?"

"I was going to blow insulation this weekend, honey. But I think it'll work for this."

"Be careful honey."

"Sure thing."

#25 Reasons

Charlie was hardly an animal enthusiast, even for dogs and cats. Still, he approached the skunk determinedly. He knew he had to be calm; he couldn't show fear.

Seth pushed past his mother to stand in the aisle with his camera phone. No way was he going to miss this. All the online videos mentioned that the skunks in them were parts of pranks, and had had their stinkers removed. Judging by the faint odor exuded by this fellow, Seth didn't think it was a prank, his dad was that lucky, or that he was going to miss an opportunity for viral video no matter what happened.

Meanwhile, Charlie wondered what words would soothe a potentially startled skunk. When a much younger Seth would fall asleep on the floor of the living room, Jane would need Charlie to put him back in bed. She couldn't pick him up without waking him. He hoped his magic touch would extend beyond his son. He channeled his inner skunk-whisperer, and, since he was already in a chapel, prayed for luck while he was at it.

The hydraulic arms that brought the casket platform up and down were not going to be his friends in this venture. A front approach was not going to work, either. He pulled his sunglasses down over his eyes – thankful the pair he'd bought was cheap and easily replaceable. He pulled the respirator up over his mouth and nose, wishing he'd opted for something a little heavier duty than the paper one he had bought. Fifteen-ninety-nine no longer sounded so expensive compared to getting a snout full of skunk odor. But he hadn't bought the suit for this, he reminded himself, and was just grateful to have what he had. Some skin on his face was still exposed, but at least his tie and jacket were off. A worthy trade, he chuckled as he'd doffed them outside the car.

Since he couldn't approach the skunk from the side, he walked to the head of the casket and crouched down.

"Great Aunt Madge," he said. "I could sure use your help more than your sense of humor right about now."

That said, he reached under the casket. He placed the beach towel on one side of the skunk. It didn't move. So he reached into the space and covered the skunk completely with the beach towel, being mindful of the business end. Then, slowly and carefully, like he's done with a sleeping Seth hundreds of times, he made a scooping motion with the beach towel and the skunk was in his arms, tail tucked under and held in place by the beach towel and Charlie's arm.

"Go Dad!" Seth cried.

"Shhh!" hissed Charlie and Jane simultaneously: Jane because they were still in the chapel, Charlie because he didn't want sudden noises to wake the animal in his arms.

#25 Reasons

"Oops. Sorry." Seth whispered. The video on the phone continued to roll.

Charlie didn't try very hard to resist walking, slightly stumbling, toward Jane's parents.

Jane's mother hissed, "Just try it, Charlie, and it's your funeral!"

"Actually," Charlie retorted. "It's Great Aunt Marjorie's." He smiled, but the mask covered most of it. His father in law tried to hide his own smirk with a bout of fake coughing. His mother in law, not fooled for a moment, elbowed him in the ribs. Charlie returned to the main aisle.

"Hey, Jane?" Charlie stage-whispered. "Back up, Seth. No need for you to get your suit sprayed."

"Aw, man! Some parents don't let their kids have any fun."

"Seth, hush. Yes, Charlie?" Jane asked, pulling Seth back into their row of seats.

"This is my last funeral, OK?"

"Whatever you say, Charlie. Thank you so much." Jane nearly had tears in her eyes, a mixture of pride, love, and fear all caught up in the female package.

"Oh, you'll thank me all right," he replied. He tried to wink at Jane, and then realized she wouldn't be able to see it through the darkened lenses. He continued his slow, solitary walk out of the chapel. Ushers opened and closed the door for him.

Everyone breathed a sigh of relief when the second door was shut. There were several moments of silence. It was broken when someone – a man, but Jane couldn't tell who it was – said aloud, "Who keeps a hazmat suit in their car?"

The comment was met with a round of laughter that made Jane furious.

"Obviously, someone not afraid to trap a skunk before it sprays all of you! Come on, Seth. Let's go help your dad."

"Now, Jane, he didn't mean…"

"Now, just a minute…"

"Jane, you have to admit…"

Jane ignored all of them. She took Seth's hand, and with head high followed her husband's path out the double doors of the chapel.

By the time Seth and Jane got outside, they saw Charlie laying the skunk, beach towel and all, at the edge of the property line. He stood up, turned around, and took a few tentative steps. Then he ran toward his wife and son.

"Dad," Seth complained. "That was my favorite beach towel."

"Do you want to go back and get it?"

#25 Reasons

Seth started toward the skunk, but Jane grabbed his arm. "No you don't, mister."

"I promise you won't like it anymore. We'll replace it in a few weeks for this summer."

"You should have put it in the house like I told you months ago when the pool closed."

"But then I would have had to use your camping blanket, Jane."

"I'm surprised you didn't try to wrap it up in your suit coat."

"I thought about it. And about tying it up with my tie. But you'd have made me replace the coat, and I don't want to spend the money on it. The beach towel is much more affordable."

Jane looked at her husband and shook her head. She may have even laughed a little, but Charlie couldn't tell.

"Do you want to go back in for the rest of the funeral?"

Seth started to tell his dad about the way his mom had stood up for him, but Jane stopped him. "No, we're good," she said. "I've paid my respects. Let's go home."

"Dad – you were awesome!"

"Son – I was lucky!"

"It would have made a better video if you'd gotten sprayed though."

"Oh, you think so?"

"Yeah, by the time I got the camera on you, it was hard to tell what you were doing, or that it was a skunk in the towel. It's not going to go viral, because nothing really exciting happened."

"Geez, son, I'm so sorry about that."

"Too bad there isn't such thing as Smell-O-Vision. Then they'd know." Seth said.

"Yes, Charlie," Jane added. "Maybe you want to think about leaving your suit with the skunk. It stinks."

Charlie pretended to misunderstand. "It shouldn't. I left my suit in the car."

"I meant…"

"He knows, Mom. He's just teasing you or something."

"Well, I'm not joking," Jane said. "You may not have been sprayed, but you still have a —" she searched for the right word — "an odor. And it will only be worse with us all cramped in the car."

Charlie compromised by tying the legs of his hazmat suit to the roof rack of the car. Because who knew if the skunk would be the only smelly or slightly dangerous thing they'd encounter before he got back to the store to replace it? If the smell did air out, then he could still use it to blow the insulation and save himself the expense of a new suit. Luckily for him, the respirators came in three packs.

They weren't ten miles down the road when Seth piped up, "Hey Dad?"

"If you're planning to ask me to get you a skunk for a pet, I'm stopping the car and you're walking home."

"Rats."

"No rats, either," retorted Jane.

"He meant," Charlie started.

"I knew exactly what he meant, Charlie. It's called a joke."

"Can I have a dog?" asked Seth.

"NO!" called both parents together.

"You two are no fun!" Seth complained.

"And don't you forget it."

You know the red pair you say I never wear anymore? Let me know you're going to read this to me, and I'll put them on. Whether or not they stay on will be up to you.

Along Came a Spider

"Charlie, wake up."

"Mmphh?"

"Charlie. Wake up. There's something on the wall."

Charlie opened a bleary eye in the direction of his alarm clock. "It's four o'clock in the morning, Jane. Why am I awake at four in the morning, Jane?"

"It just moved!" Jane whispered in a panicked voice. "Oh, Charlie. I think it's a spider. Please -- kill it for me."

"It is poisonous?"

"It has eight legs." Jane offered, still clearly panicking. She could handle nosebleeds, monster movies, worms, and rodents. She drew the line at spiders. She pulled her part of the blankets up around her as she sat up in bed, knees under chin, like a child afraid of monsters in the closet. "Oh, Charlie, it's moving. I think it hears me."

"Do you think it hears me?"

"Maybe." Jane's voice quivered hopefully.

"Good." Charlie addressed the spider, "Hey spider. If you promise not to bite us and let me sleep, I'll let you live. How's that sound?" Then he cocked his head, as though listening to the spider's response. He turned to Jane. "The

197

spider says it sounds like a plan. It's just going to check out a few dust mites over there and hopes we didn't mind." He turned back to the spider. "We don't mind at all. You go right ahead and explore those dust mites. Hope they're delicious."

Jane was not amused. "Charlie! You can't reason with a spider! And you can't leave it there. I won't be able to sleep. Charlie, please. Charlie." Jane sobbed hysterically.

"Jane, do you know what the odds are of that spider crawling up the wall, onto the ceiling, dropping onto you, biting you, and killing you?"

"No." Jane paused, expecting an answer. None came. "What are the odds?"

"I don't know either. Can't be very good. Would you just go back to sleep?"

"I can't. Charlie, you know I can't."

"Yeah. I know. It was worth a shot, though." Charlie swung his legs over the side of the bed and stretched. He was getting too old for this. He turned on the lamp next to his bed and pointed it toward the wall.

"Where is this behemoth spider that disturbed your slumber and therefore mine?"

"Over there. In the corner. About twelve inches above your elbow."

#25 Reasons

"Oh, this little guy? Uh, girl? Uh, spider?" Charlie carefully picked the spider up by a leg and let it crawl from palm to palm. "It's just a wolf spider. See this cat eye on the top? She's a beauty." Jane wasn't sure if Charlie really liked spiders, or if he just liked to torment her. "You're harmless, aren't you Octaleggia? Yes, you are. And so cute."

"It's a spider, not a puppy, Charlie."

"I know. Dogs have fleas. Spiders, however, eat fleas. I prefer the spiders."

"What are you going to do with it?"

"I guess I have to flush it. Give it a fighting chance to live." Charlie turned toward their bathroom suite door.

"No Charlie! Spiders can swim. I don't want it coming back up the toilet bowl and biting me while I'm trying to pee in the morning."

"Well, then I'm really sorry, Madame Octaleggia. But Jane gets what Jane"

"Stop, Charlie! You can't just smash it now. Can't you just put it outside or something? Something humane? I mean, you just named it."

So Charlie carried the little wolf spider to the window ledge, opened the window, and placed the spider on the screen. Then he shut the window.

"Lock it, please."

"But Jane," Charlie protested. "What if Madame Octaleggia has a key?"

"You goof. Would you just lock the window?"

"As you wish, my lady. As you wish."

C --

Honestly – I love that you're even reading this. It does show me you still care.

J

Mother's Day

While Jane feigned sleep upstairs, Seth and Charlie manned up to create breakfast in bed, flowers, and a card for her.

"Seth!" Charlie tried to keep his voice down while still getting his son's attention. Get up and get in the car. We've got to get Mother's Day sorted for your mom."

"Must sleep. Five more minutes."

"We don't have five minutes, son. Your mom is going to think we forgot."

"We did forget."

"We don't want her knowing that!"

"What's the big deal? Mother's Day is made up by the card and chocolate companies, anyway." Seth had heard his dad say this all the time, so he thought it was a brownie point worth scoring with his old man.

"Yeah, and I will be happy to agree with you after we've made your mother's perfect, so come on!"

Seth struggled to a sitting position and grabbed the trousers he'd kicked to the foot of the bed the night before. They passed the sniff test, so he struggled into them again. "What's been the deal with you and Mom, anyway? You go

203

to work. I go to school. She stays home. I don't get what the big deal is."

"She lets you live, son, after you open your mouth and dumb stuff like that falls out. What about that huge fundraiser she put together for your school?"

"That was ages ago, Dad."

"Tell that to the kids who are going to pay less for college because of the scholarships that fundraiser made."

"Yeah, yeah, yeah. But, still, I don't get it. What's the big deal?"

"You don't have to get it, son. Get moving."

Ten minutes later, they were in the car.

"I used to make mom breakfast. Why are we going someplace?"

"Donuts. And we're out of eggs to go with the bacon. And flowers and card."

"We have to get her a card?"

"Don't worry. I'll pick out two and the flowers. You can get the donuts and the groceries. We'll meet at the registers as soon as possible."

"Should I get her some chocolate, too?"

"If you value your life."

"Ok. Eggs, bacon, donuts, chocolate. Got it. Anything else?"

"Might want to get small cartons of milk and OJ."

#25 Reasons

"Geez. I'm not sure if I'll remember all that stuff."

"You could make a list on your phone."

"No way! That's what Mom does. You don't do that."

"I don't need to do that."

"But sometimes you forget stuff."

"You have an unfortunate habit of opening your mouth when you really shouldn't – you know that?"

Seth ignored this. "Dad?"

"Guess not." Charlie muttered under his breath. "What is it, son?"

"I still want to know what the deal is with you and Mom. I asked her and she said you're not getting a divorce, so why do you care if she's happy or not?"

Charlie hit the brakes so hard the car behind honked and swerved to avoid a collision. He wiped his mouth with his hand, a gesture Seth had come to recognize as part thinking and part not saying the swear-word he wanted.

"Sorry, Dad. I didn't mean anything bad. I'm on your side."

Charlie took his foot off the brake and drove in silence to the store. When he pulled in and parked, he took several deep breaths. Seth pressed himself into the car door, uncertain what was coming next.

"Seth." Charlie said after what felt to Seth like a very long time. "I love your mother."

"I know, Dad."

"I'm not sure you do. And you're young yet. You haven't been in love yet. But when you love someone enough to marry 'em, to have crazy-good- for-nothing kids with 'em, you want them to be happy. Your mom is my best friend. She's unhappy. It's my job to fix it."

"But why?"

"Because there's nobody I'd rather have my back than your mom. She keeps the house running. She knows where all our lost things end up. She lets you screw up doing things around the house and puts up with your complaining so that when you're ready to date you can fool some girl into thinking you're an evolved gentlemen instead of the half-ape your mother and I know and love. I didn't do that – your mom did. My mom did that for me. My mom was my best friend until the day she died. And until I met your mom, I didn't think I'd ever have that again."

Seth just sat there, stunned.

"On our anniversary," Charlie ticked off the events with his fingers, "on her birthday, and on Mother's Day, Mom gets a little emotional and wants to be pampered a bit. I screwed up her birthday. I am getting this right."

Seth sighed. "Ok, Dad. I love Mom, too, you know."

"I know. Sometimes I think you love her more than me."

#25 Reasons

"Well, yeah. She gets me. And soon I'm going to be taller than she is."

"See, there your mouth goes, getting you into trouble again."

Out of the car and on the way into the store, Seth surprised Charlie with a hug. Charlie hugged back.

"I love you, too, Dad. Not just Mom."

"Ok," said a choked-up Charlie. This young man was so much Jane's doing. He owed her big-time.

They walked into the store together, but quickly separated to their own tasks. Remembering a trick of Jane's, Charlie texted "eggs, bacon, milk, OJ, donuts, chocolate" to Seth's phone. He vowed to use the list next time before Jane went shopping again. He could be a good example for Seth. And he had to admit it would help him to have a list, too – he wasn't as young as he used to be, and there was a lot on his mind most days besides groceries.

Sunday morning on Mother's Day, the greeting card aisle was pretty well picked over, but Charlie found two that would work – one to be from Seth, and one that better not be from Seth – in among the graduation money holders. Why graduation weekend fell on Mother's Day weekend would never fail to baffle him. It was hard enough remembering without other things being added to it. But Seth wouldn't graduate for a few more years yet, so one less thing to worry about.

Cards in hand, Charlie went to the floral cooler. It looked even worse than the greeting card aisle. He smartly bypassed the sad remains of thorny roses and selected instead a larger glass vase with purple and yellow tulips.

"Can I help you find something?" A woman's voice made Charlie turn. "Oh, I see. I'm sorry for your loss, sir."

"They're for my wife. For Mother's Day." Then Charlie looked down at the ribbon that adorned the floral vase. "With deepest sympathy," he read. "Geez. That's just perfect."

"Sir? Sir! I don't think you understand."

"I don't. Never will. But she already knows that. Thanks!" The poor employee was dumbfounded. Charlie took his find and met his son at the registers.

"With deepest sympathy." Seth read. "Are we really that bad?"

"Worse. Besides, son, you can never be too careful when it comes to your mother's special day."

Author's Note

About the Ending(s)

There were two obvious ways that this book could end without Charlie and Jane parting ways. Now, sometimes that happens, but that is not this story.

This story ends with Charlie realizing that Jane can't just accept the lump of clay that he sees as himself. He's a living, breathing human being. To love who Jane is means loving that she demands the most and best out of those she loves. Complacency will never be an option for Jane. If she ever didn't care, then he should be worried about separation or divorce. Charlie will always be worth it to Jane – whether he appreciates it or not. And because he's Charlie, and she's Jane, he does.

Jane can appreciate that Charlie married her hoping that the girl he thought he fooled, cajoled, and duped into marrying him wouldn't change – that she would stay fooled, cajoled, and duped for as long they both should live. But Jane did change. Age changed her. Marriage changed her. Motherhood changed her. Even with just one kid, Jane was surrounded by children – hers, her friends', her co-workers', and her son's friends. And those kids and their parents led Jane to consider many "what if" scenarios

211

Phyl Campbell

at various stages of her life. What if Seth had brothers and sisters? What if Seth got a girl pregnant before he got his driver's license? What if she had been able to find a job and was working all the time – would Seth have still turned out ok? Will he be ok because she didn't? Jane's decisions were challenged over and over. Every decision was judged, and this judgment caused her to change.

Jane married Charlie hoping for someone to grow and grow old with her. And somehow, this only happen to Charlie in physical characteristics like failing senses, wrinkles, or hair loss. Maybe a few extra pounds. He's still the goofy Charlie she married. That occasionally insufferable boyishness is charming in its own way – what woman doesn't want a guy who can make her laugh? As long as Jane can remember THAT (and that she looks horrible both in stripes and in prison orange), she and Charlie (and Seth) will be ok. Jane learns to accept that some of her problems with Charlie have very little to do with Charlie; they're about her life. Chick flicks and dramas and romance novels provide her an escape for a little while – everyone needs some form of escape from time to time. Expecting someone from Mars to understand someone from Venus may be asking a bit too much. And planetary collisions can be fun, right?

#25 Reasons

For all the Charlies (and also many women, but for different reasons), this book would not satisfy until Jane got those filthy, disgusting rags (all the romance novels) out of her house. So read the first ending and be satisfied.

The second ending, however, allows for Charlie and Jane to accept each other's differences and just be different together. I liked the idea of Charlie and Jane ending the book in bed. I hope you will, too.

Personally, I doubt I've ever been accused of being a girly-girl, a Southern Belle, or anything like that. I do like the occasional chick-lit novel. They have interesting quirks. They aren't going to make me too scared or grossed out to sleep. They tend to have well-developed characters in typical towns doing some soul-searching and hopefully growing in the process. And – don't get me wrong -- sometimes the romps in the sheets are fun to read, too.

So whether reading the first ending, the second, or like me, reading both and alternating between the two depending on mood, know that you probably picked this book up because someone you love dearly also quite often makes you want to scream – and not always in ecstasy. It's ok. Men and women worldwide are with you. Eventually, it's all funny, even though this may be one of those occasions where it's only funny UNTIL you can relate or enough time has passed to see the humor behind the groaning.

Enough from me – finish the story!

25 Reasons (1st Ending)

Jane loved Charlie. She still didn't know for sure whether her brilliant husband was at times a Y-chromosomed- imbecile, or if he was just playing the part, but right then, Jane just didn't care. She gathered all her favorite romance novels in a paper bag – ok, so it took two – and thanked several deities that she had not marked her name on most of them. These were the novels she had bought second and third-hand as dirty pleasures, books she needed to be able to deny having bought for herself, books that she had been too embarrassed to include in her own yard sales.

Now, the thought that some other couple might have tried to use these books to add spice to their own bedroom lives – Jane couldn't remove them from her home fast enough. To think there were people who got their romance novels and erotica from the public library – her every sense shuddered at the thought. How many times had *Thirty-three Shades of Erotic Blue Pills* been checked out, read, and experimented with? How much lube stuck those pages together? Never again would she join patrons on the waiting list for books like that.

Phyl Campbell

Fridays were good days for neighborhood yard sales in her cul de sac, and it didn't take long for Jane to find an elderly neighbor setting one up with boxes already marked "books: twenty-five cents each."

"Hey, do you want some more books for your sale?" Jane asked.

"Are they textbooks? I never can get rid of those."

"No. They're romance." Jane said with a hint of a smile.

"Romance, you say?" The elderly neighbor's eyes lit up. "Well, well -- pull up a chair."

The older woman indicated a pair of folding camping chair near to the garage door. She sat as well, and wiped her sweaty brow with a rag she had around her shoulders. "I keep the both out here for when the mister wants to gawk, but he's still reading the paper this morning. But now, tell me, what kind of romance books do you got there?"

"Only a little of this and a little of that." Jane teased.

The old woman picked one up. "I've heard of this author. Is she any good?"

Without batting an eye, Jane said "Sure, if you're a self-starter."

#25 Reasons

The old woman hooted and slapped her knee. "Honey," she said conspiratorially, "how in the world do you think I've stayed with him forty-two years?"

Jane had forgotten how good it felt to laugh.

"Now, if you don't mind, I'm gonna put this one back for myself, but you see those ladies with the tennis skirts?"

Jane nodded.

"They're young wives. They don't hav any kids yet. They've been coming to me for the saucy stuff for months now. I started going to the library discard sales to keep 'em coming to me. Today I got a little more than usual, I guess. And what they don't want today, I might read or they might come back for."

"Glad I could help. So you do this all the time?"

"As often as I feel like."

"I thought there was a limit on yard sales."

"There is. But I'm just a frail old woman and my memory's gone. Surely I didn't have a sale last week. I'm not rich, you know."

The way the woman mocked herself talking to law enforcement reminded Jane of all the times she imagined having to do the same thing. Play dumb, and live to play another day. People should be insulted how well it worked on authority figures.

"Should I pay you? For the books?"

217

"What?" Jane snapped out of her reverie. "Oh. The books. Gosh, no. Please. Get what you can out of them. They were just taking up space in my house."

The neighbor nodded, as if deciding something. "Good girl. You're a good girl." She said. Then she patted Jane on the knee, rose, and turned to the women in the tennis skirts. "Just sit tight a minute. Oh girls! Have I got something for you!"

The grown women giggled in response and hurried over to examine the older woman's wares. At first, Jane was happy to see them smiling and giggling over the racy covers. But then, a feeling came over Jane. Suddenly, she was embarrassed to be there. She grunted and got out of the low camping chair and started on her way home.

"Wait a minute, honey!"

"Yes, ma'am?" Jane turned back around to her neighbor.

"I get kinda lonely puttering around the house with just the mister. What do you say to the idea of kidnapping me in that car of yours one day next week? I don't drive a whole lot these days."

"Excuse me?"

"Once your boy is safely on his way to school, come over and we'll plan some grand lady adventure. I think it would be good for both of us. Don't you?"

"Well, sure, I mean – of course. I'd be happy to"

"Everybody needs somebody to talk to – I think you might be just who I've been looking for. Just tell me you'll consider it."

"I will, ma'am."

"Call me Emma."

"Yes, ma'am. Emma, I mean. I'm Jane."

can you
make me
drop my
book?

25 Reasons (2nd Ending)

"Put the book down for a minute." Charlie put the book down. "Now, how is someone not being read to going to follow these instructions?" He and Jane were in bed at the end of a very long week. But he had promised to read to her, and here he was, keeping that promise. However reluctantly.

"They get the audio version. Please. Just read it to me."

"Fine." Charlie went back to the book. "Close your eyes. Imagine your lover taking hold of your hand. Your lover knows how you want to be touched. Every caress is perfect."

He looked over at Jane. Her eyes were closed and he could see the little wrinkles around her crow's feet start to relax. He kept reading.

"Imagine there – just there – you know the spot. Right there is a firm touch. And then there – right there – fingers soft as feathers caress your skin. Nothing but sensations -- perfect sensations – cross your mind. All you want to do is feel. The sensations build. They build. They build. And right where you are, you can't control yourself. You release into the perfection of sensation."

Charlie couldn't stop himself. He put down the book again.

"What's wrong, Charlie?" Jane asked, speech slightly slurred from her relaxed near-sleep state.

"This book is crap. A spontaneous orgasm like that can't just happen. You have to actually be having sex." Charlie argued, disgusted.

"How would you know?" Jane demanded.

Charlie noticed Jane's crow's feet stood out when she was angry. He thought it best not to mention it to her. Instead, he tried to say something comforting.

"We've made it good, baby. And you've never had a reaction like that to me taking your hand."

This was clearly the wrong thing to say.

"So because you've never made me feel like that, it can't happen."

"Exactly."

Wasn't it?

"Because YOU are the best lover there is."

"I'm the best you've ever had."

Jane scoffed. "What about Don Juan de Marco?"

#25 Reasons

"Don't bring your previous boyfriends into this. We've been married too long for me to be jealous of any of them."

Charlie didn't remember Jane dating a Juan. He made a note to ask Amy about it at some point.

Jane crossed her arms over her chest and took several deep breaths.

"Give me the damn book."

Charlie was only too happy to comply.

"You know it's not about this, right Charlie?" Jane said.

Charlie was trying to understand, but he didn't. He could tell that Jane was trying not to cry, so he knew he'd screwed up again.

"Never mind." Jane said. But Charlie could tell that she did mind. And it really wasn't that big of a deal.

"I'm sorry, Jane. I'll do better. Here. I'll finish that page. Lie back down here and shut your eyes."

"But this is just stupid to you."

"And it is a stupid book." Charlie agreed. "But I have a way to make it better."

Charlie gave it his best shot. He knew he was on the right track when Jane let go of the book and it fell on the floor. No one was in a hurry to pick it up.

No one's looking:
want to take a page
from the book of
Charlie and Jane?

Go ahead – you know
you want to.
Besides,
who's going to know?
You don't kiss and tell,
do you?

About the Author

Phyl Campbell has been scribbling dialogue on pieces of paper ever since she was old enough to hold a pencil. Like Jane, she's somewhat notorious for lists. When neither writing nor thinking up diabolical plots to take over the world, Phyl enjoys spending time online, curled up with a book, creating music, with her spouse and son, or teaching. She appreciates your questions and comments. "Like" her Phyl Campbell Author Page on Facebook, visit her webpage www.phylcampbell.com, or follow her on Twitter @phylc_author.